MANDIE
AND THE
SECRET
TUNNEL

MANDIE
AND THE
SECRET
TUNNEL

Lois Gladys Leppard

BETHANY HOUSE PUBLISHERS
MINNEAPOLIS, MINNESOTA 55438
A Division of Bethany Fellowship, Inc.

Library of Congress Catalog Card Number 82-74053

ISBN 0-87123-320-7

Published by Bethany House Publishers
A Division of Bethany Fellowship, Inc.
6820 Auto Club Road, Minneapolis, Minnesota 55438

Printed in the United States of America

For My Mother,
Bessie A. Wilson Leppard,
and
In Memory of Her Sister,
Lillie Margaret Ann Wilson Frady,
Orphans of North Carolina
Who Outgrew the Sufferings of Childhood

About the Author

LOIS GLADYS LEPPARD has been a Federal Civil Service employee in various countries around the world. The stories of her own mother's childhood are the basis for many of the incidents incorporated in this series.

Table of Contents

Books in this series:

*"The Lord is my shepherd,
I shall not want—"*

Chapter 1 / Mandie

"Don't get so close, Amanda. You might fall in." Her mother grasped the back of her long, dark skirt.

Mandie tried to pull free. Her tear-filled blue eyes sought a glimpse of her father through the homemade wooden coffin resting by the open grave.

"I want to go with you, Daddy!" she was mumbling to herself. "Take me with you, Daddy!" she tugged at her long, blonde braid in her grief.

Even in her sadness she was afraid of being scolded by her stern mother. She dared not cry out in anguish. Her voice trembled as she whispered, "How can I live without you, Daddy? You were the only one who ever loved me. I can't bear it alone!"

Preacher DeHart's deep voice echoed throughout the hills. "We all know Jim Shaw was a good man. He drew his last breath talking to God. We trust his soul is at peace."

His voice grew louder and more emphatic. "But, friends and loved ones, I am here to remind you of one thing! When the time comes for you to face your Maker, you will be damned to hellfire and brimstone if you have lived a sinful life!"

Mandie trembled as she heard the words.

"You will incur the wrath of God and your soul will burn in hell forevermore," he continued. "Above all, let us remember the Ten Command-ments and keep them holy, live by them and walk the straight and narrow path in preparation for the hereafter. Otherwise, I admonish you, your soul will burn in hell! Your soul will be used to feed the fires of the devil! When you have sinned and come short of the glory of God, He will forsake you. He will pun-ish you!"

The child was overcome by fear and grief as the final words were said for her father and the cof-fin was lowered into the ground. The clods of mountain woods dirt hit the casket with a thud. She gasped for breath and, falling on her knees beside the grave, she appealed to God, "What have I done to cause you to take my daddy away, dear God? You know I can't live without my daddy, God. I love him so much, dear God!"

The crowd standing nearby silently wiped away tears. The earth was smoothed into a mound and a rough marker was pounded into the soil with an axe. It read, "James Alexander Shaw; Born April 3, 1863; Died April 13, 1900." Such a small remembrance for such a big-hearted man. Jim Shaw had no enemies. Everyone had been his friend.

It was April, but it was still cold in the Nantahala Mountains of North Carolina. Mandie, trembling with cold and emotion, couldn't stop shaking enough to rise from her knees, so her mother grabbed her arm and pulled her up and away from her father's grave. Her legs would hardly carry her.

Through her blinding tears she caught a glimpse of Uncle Ned standing at the edge of the woods. Uncle Ned, the old Cherokee Indian, came often to the Shaws' neighborhood selling hand-woven baskets. He and Mandie's father had been good friends. He had loved her father, too. She suddenly jerked free from her mother, running to the tall Indian for comfort. Uncle Ned stooped to catch her in his arms, his necklace of shells softly brushing against her face.

"Uncle Ned, God doesn't love me anymore! He took my daddy away from me!" she cried.

"My papoose! Father—good man. Not gone far—only to happy hunting ground." His pronunciation was good, but his grammar was poor. He stroked her blonde hair as she buried her wet face against his deerskin jacket.

"Amanda, come now. We're goin' home. Right now!" The plump woman shouted to the girl. "Come, git in the wagon!"

"Uncle Ned, please come to see me. I love

you." Mandie quickly kissed his redskinned cheek and turned to obey her mother.

The old Indian held her hand. "I make promise—your father. I look out for you. I keep promise." He smiled and released her hand.

Her heartbeat quickened as she heard his words. There would be someone to watch over her. But Uncle Ned could never overrule her mother; she had always bossed her father around. But then, Uncle Ned had his whole tribe behind him! He would indeed keep his word to her father.

Etta Shaw snatched the girl's hand and slapped her face. "Hesh up! Git in the wagon! This minute!" She gave the girl a shove and called instructions to her sister.

Mandie's sister, Irene, all but lifted her up as she forced the girl to climb into the waiting wagon, the same one that had brought her father's casket to the cemetery. All the other mourners had already turned down the long hill ahead of them.

"Now set down and shet up!" Irene was two years older, and eleven-year-old Mandie was afraid of her rough ways. She knew she couldn't resist. She gave one last pitiful look at Uncle Ned, who stood witnessing the scene with his keen black eyes, and fixed her gaze ahead.

She would go home now, but she would come back as soon as she got the chance. Her eyes stayed on the mound of earth until they were down the side of the mountain and the row of trees blocked her view.

Sitting in the back of the wagon with her sister, Mandie suddenly realized that her mother had not shed a tear. Neither had her sister. She turned to look at her mother. Etta Shaw was busily talking and laughing with Zach as they bumped on down the rough road. She didn't love my daddy, she was thinking. She acts like she's glad he's gone. How could she laugh as though she had already forgotten he ever existed?

Her thoughts turned back to the happy times with her father. He was always laughing, always ready to take her side in any disagreement with her mother and Irene. She could see his smiling face, his red curly hair, his blue eyes twinkling with some little secret between them. He had always been there to comfort his dear Mandie through the trials and tribulations of her eleven years, and then suddenly he was gone. God had taken him away.

Mandie was beginning to realize the way things really were. She could never remember being loved by her mother. Young as she was, she knew Irene was her mother's favorite. As far back as she could recall, Irene had always been given the new dresses which were later shortened to fit her, even though the dresses were made with rows of tucks around the skirts that could have been let out as Irene grew. She had never had a brand new dress in her life. The old, dark blue frock she was wearing had been made for Irene and, although it was almost threadbare, it had been hemmed yesterday for her to wear to her father's funeral. Mandie tugged at the faded fabric wishing she could be rid of the dress.

"Why don't they hurry up and get home?" she cried to herself. Her mother and Zach were leisurely riding along, talking too low for Mandie to understand what they were saying, with an occasional loud laugh from her mother. Irene kept herself busy snatching at the bushes as the wagon brushed past them on the narrow dirt road.

At last they got down to Charley Gap and their log cabin came into sight. It was huddled in the trees at the bottom of the slope. The hill to the north behind it gave protection against the cold mountain winds in the winter. The clearing around the house was already full of wagons and buggies and horses. People were standing around talking under the chestnut trees. Zach drove their wagon straight to the barn.

Mandie knew she would never be able to escape her mother that day. She would have to help wait on all these people who had come to eat and drink as soon as her father had been laid out in the front room on Friday. Today being Sunday, the whole congregation had come after the church services, which had included the last rites for her father. She knew none of them had been home yet to eat and that meant work for her. She had never been near a death before and she couldn't understand why they all acted like it was a party. Why don't they all go home and leave me alone? she wondered. I want to be by myself and think.

The chickens clucked and scattered as her

mother jumped down from the wagon. "Let's git to the kitchen and see about the vittles."

She waited to see that Mandie was coming along behind her. Mandie scooped up her fluffy white kitten, who had come to greet her, and ran toward the house.

"See you in a little while, Zach. Gotta git this crowd fed. Better come on up and git something to eat yourself," Etta called back.

"Be along in a minute, Etta." Zach spit tobacco juice as he replied and began unharnessing Molly.

Irene jumped down from the wagon as a tall, gangly boy came up. She put on her best smile and smoothed her skirts as she tossed her dark hair.

"Hello, Nimrod," she giggled. "Wanta take a walk up to the springhouse 'fore Ma puts me to work?"

"Shore, Irene," the boy answered eagerly. "Druther slip off any day than work. Let's go git a long, cool drink of that sprang water."

The two hurried off behind the cabin before Etta missed Irene.

As Mandie walked through the crowd in the front room, she saw old Mrs. Shope take a dip of snuff, stick her sweetgum toothbrush in her tooth-less mouth, and then remark, "Poor child. He was all she had. Things is goin' to be rough now for all of 'em."

Mrs. DeWeese shook her gray head. "No, not so long as that thar Zach Hughes is around." She smiled a knowing grin.

Mandie fled through the door into the kitchen, not wanting to hear anymore, and, above all, not wanting to speak to any of these people. They were mostly her mother's kinfolk and friends. This was her mother's part of the country. Her father had always told her his people lived a long way off, but he had never said where.

The big, round oak table was loaded with food the people had brought, but it held no enticement to her nervous stomach. The warmth from the wood cookstove felt good to her. The heat thawed her somewhat and she wanted to talk.

"Mama," she began, unsure of herself, "where did my daddy come from?"

Etta Shaw stopped to look at her and she set down the plates from the cupboard. "What do you mean, where did he come from?"

"Well, you always said he was raised in a city somewhere—"

"That's right," Etta interrupted. "He was book read. That's all'n you need to know. Now git all the knives and forks out, and the glasses. We'll be needin' all of 'em. And run git that first piece of ham hanging on the right side in the smokehouse."

Mandie gave a sigh and obeyed. She longed for the day to end.

*"He maketh me to lie
down in green pastures—"*

Chapter 2 / Mandie Leaves Home

The full moon was coming up between the hills
of Charley Gap as Mandie sat on the doorstep,
wrapped in the quilt from her bed.

All the people had finally left and she, her
mother and Irene had gone to bed. She had listened, as she lay there on her cornshuck mattress,
to be sure they were asleep, and then cuddling
Snowball, her kitten, she had climbed down the ladder from the attic room where she slept with her
sister. She couldn't go to sleep.

She was thinking of her past and wondering
about her future without her father. She was remembering Preacher DeHart's words about God,
"He will punish you!" What had she done wrong?
Why was she being punished?

A soft whistle that sounded like a bird came

17

from the nearby trees. She rose quickly as she saw Uncle Ned coming toward her, his soft moccasins soundless.

She ran to meet him, dragging the quilt and dropping Snowball. "Oh, Uncle Ned! I'm so glad you came!"

"I come find story why Jim Shaw go to happy hunting ground."

The old man put his arm around the child as they sat down on a nearby log.

"He had a bad cold, Uncle Ned, a real bad cold, and it just got worse."

"Cold?" The old Indian did not understand.

"Yes. Mama said it was new—ah—new moanie. He—he told me—he told me he was going to Heaven—that he would wait for me there." She broke into sobs.

"Don't make tears, Papoose. He wait. He always keeps promise." Uncle Ned wiped her eyes with the corner of the quilt. "When he go?"

"Today is Sunday. It was day before yesterday, Friday. Oh, why did he leave me? Why couldn't I go with him?"

"You little papoose now. Must be big squaw first. Big God, He say when you come. We do what He say. Remember? Jim Shaw, he tell us about Big God. Cherokee believe him. Jim Shaw one of our people."

She turned quickly to look at him. "My father, one of your people? But my father was a white man—red hair, blue eyes—and you are an Indian!"

"Yes. And his father look same. Your daddy never want tell you his Mama Indian squaw. Him one of our people. Him—"

Mandie interrupted excitedly, "My grandmother was an Indian? Are you really my Uncle Ned?"

"Jim Shaw—one brother. He never come see. Jim Shaw take me for brother."

"Is my grandmother still living?"

"No, she go to happy hunting ground when Jim Shaw little brave."

"What about my grandfather? Is he living?"

"I do not know. Jim Shaw never tell me when he come to see Cherokee."

"My daddy used to come to see you? Where do you live, Uncle Ned?"

"Over the hills. That way." He pointed toward one of the hills above the cabin. "Follow Nantahala River."

"Could I come to see you sometime?"

"No, bear get Papoose. Wolf, panther wait for Papoose to come."

"But they don't get you."

"I shoot with arrow." He patted the sling over his shoulder holding his huge witch hazel bow and his arrows with turkey feathers. "I kill."

"I've never been anywhere except to school and to church. The schoolhouse is just down the road apiece, and we go in the wagon to church at Maple Springs. And all the Sunday school teacher ever says is 'Honor thy mother and thy father,' and all that stuff. I never can remember the rest of it.

Uncle Ned, do you think God really means for us to honor our mother?"

"Big Book say that?"

"Yes, that's what it says, the Bible."

"Then you do what it say. Jim Shaw say, we don't do what Big Book say, we don't get see Big God."

"But my mother—" she hesitated.

"I know. I see. I hear. She bad squaw."

The girl smiled at his description. "Even if she is bad, do I still have to honor her?"

"Book say that?"

"The Bible doesn't say whether your mother has to be good or bad. It just says honor thy mother."

"Then close ears, eyes. Honor mother." Uncle Ned stood up. "Papoose go sleep now. I come again soon. Go now."

Mandie scrambled to her feet and picked up Snowball, who was rubbing around her feet. She would go back to bed, but now she would have other things to think about. She was part Cherokee Indian! Why had her father never told her? If she could get enough courage, she would ask her mother about it.

Back in her bed, with Snowball curled up by her side, she finally fell asleep. Her mother woke her, yelling from downstairs. It was morning, but Mandie felt as though she had just closed her eyes.

"Git up, Amanda. Work to be done. Amanda, you hear me?"

"Yes, Mama." She sat up. Irene was still asleep. She reached over and shook her sister. "Irene, Mama is up."

"Leave me alone. I'm not ready to git up yet." Irene pulled the cover over her head.

Mandie quickly dressed in the early morning chill, remembering cold mornings when she was small and her father had held her in his lap by the fireplace downstairs while he put on her shoes and stockings.

Then she remembered her conversation with Uncle Ned. Maybe she could catch her mother in the right mood if she hurried and she could ask some questions about what Uncle Ned had told her. But when she reached the last rung of the ladder, her mother was waiting for her with the milk bucket.

"Go milk Susie while I start breakfast. Git a move on," Etta Shaw scolded.

Without a word, Mandie took the bucket, set Snowball down as she went outside and raced with the kitten to the barn. She didn't mind Susie at all. Susie was her friend. She always stood still and made mooing sounds while Mandie milked her, but when her mother tried it, Susie kicked up a fuss and would turn the bucket over if she got a chance. She would also use her tail to slap Etta Shaw in the face. Only Jim and Mandie were able to handle her and now that her father was gone, she could see the job falling entirely upon her.

"Good morning, Susie." She rubbed the cow's

head. "You gonna give me a good bucketful of milk this morning? If you don't, Mama will scold me and I want to get her in a good mood so I can find out some things." She drew up the little three-legged stool. Susie looked back at her and began her mooing, and the bucket was soon full to the brim.

"Thank you, Susie. Now I'll let the bars down so you can get outside and get your breakfast. Please don't go too far away, because I know I'll have to come and get you tonight." The cow moved out into the pasture. She set the milk bucket down and followed. It was such a beautiful spring morning. Her eyes roamed over the fields, seeing her father as she remembered him and she fell to her knees on the soft, green grass.

"Dear God, please take good care of my daddy," she implored. "And, dear God, I still love you even if you don't love me anymore."

She hurried back to the house, certain that her mother would be pleased to see so much milk, but she only took the bucket and set it on the sideboard.

"Git a move on, Amanda. School today, as usual." Going to the ladder, she called, "Irene, git up. Breakfast is ready. School today."

Mandie sat down to her grits and biscuits with honey without another word. She kept staring at her father's empty place at the table. She could see it was no time to talk to her mother.

Irene joined her and then they prepared their

lunch in baskets their father had bought from Uncle Ned. They put in sausage and biscuits, and buttermilk in tightly closed jars which would be warm by the time recess came at school. They took their sunbonnets down from the pegs by the door, tied them on and together they began their mile-long walk down the road to the one-room schoolhouse. Even Irene was glad to get away from her mother to enjoy the company of her classmates.

There were only sixteen pupils in the school and one teacher, Mr. Tallant. They were divided into four groups of four, one group in each corner of the big schoolroom. Mr. Tallant would go from group to group giving assignments, listening to reading, and recitation of arithmetic. He was not a strict schoolmaster and as long as a student made good grades he pretended not to notice the passing of notes during the time they were reading to themselves.

Mandie frequently received notes written in poetry from Joe Woodard, whose father was the only doctor in the vicinity. Joe had been her best friend from the day she had begun school, young, shy, and bewildered. Joe was two years older, an experienced hand in the schoolroom, and he immediately took Mandie under his protection. Irene was jealous and made life miserable for the boy.

Joe passed a folded note to Mandie with the explanation that he had had to return home with his mother after her father's funeral because his father, the doctor, had to make some urgent sick calls.

Even though he lived a good two miles from the Shaws, he showed up there quite often. Etta Shaw tried her best to get him interested in Irene, but Joe had eyes only for Mandie. His note told her that he had permission to walk home with her, and his father would pick him up on his way home.

The two strolled along the road, ignoring Irene who tagged by the side. Joe carried Mandie's books and she tried to listen to his attempt to cheer her up, but her thoughts kept reverting to the fact that her father would not be home when she got there. Her father usually finished the many chores around the farm by the time school was over each day and almost always lately he would be splitting logs at the chopping block for the fence he planned to put around the property. She knew this would take quite a while because the farm had one hundred and twenty acres. The pile had steadily grown and he had begun hauling the rails around the boundary line a few days before he became ill.

"I'm sure glad to feel the weather getting warmer," Joe remarked, throwing back his thin shoulders and taking a deep breath. "When hot weather comes I always feel better, for some reason."

"I never thought about it," Mandie remarked. "Yeh, I suppose I like hot weather better, too, even though there are spiders and bugs and snakes crawling around."

"I ain't afraid of them things. I'm bigger than they are," Irene put in.

"You might be bigger, but you'd still better not fool around with snakes," Joe told her.

"That's why Daddy planted the gourds, to keep the snakes away from the house," Mandie added.

"Yeh, I know," Joe said. "Here comes Snowball. It's a miracle to me how that kitten knows when you're coming home."

"He's smart. He always knows." Mandie stopped to pick up the kitten. "He knows when it's time to go to bed, too. He waits for me at the ladder every night."

As they walked into the yard, Etta Shaw saw them coming and was waiting to give out the chores.

"Change your dress, Mandie. The yard needs sweeping after all that mob of wagons and people here yesterday," and turning to Irene, she said, "You can churn the milk, Irene."

Mandie hurried upstairs and changed into her old faded dress and came back down to find Joe waiting with the broom in his hand.

"I'll help," he told her. "You pick up the trash, papers, and things around and I'll do the sweeping. We'll get it done in no time."

"Thanks, Joe," Mandie said.

The rough handmade broom always made blisters on her hands and then when she had to wash dishes her hands would feel like they were on fire.

She ran about collecting papers, moving rocks out of the way that had been used to prop wagon wheels. Joe swept furiously and they were soon finished.

Etta Shaw came to the front door with the

water bucket. She took the gourd dipper out of the pail and handed it to Mandie. "Fetch me some water. And then take this bucket of slop down to the hog walla." She indicated another bucket sitting in the doorway.

So, between Mandie and Joe they brought the water from the spring and then went to feed the pigs. By that time, Dr. Woodard was pulling up in his buggy.

"And how are you today, Mandie?" the doctor greeted the girl.

"Fine, Dr. Woodard." She smiled shyly at the old man.

"Come in, Dr. Woodard," Etta yelled from the doorway. "You younguns come in, too. We'll have a piece of that pound cake Mrs. Shope brought yesterday."

"I only want a glass of sweetmilk," Mandie told her. She didn't want anything that would remind her of yesterday.

"Well, Etta, what are you going to do now?" Dr. Woodard asked, as they all sat at the round table in the kitchen.

"Marry the first man that'll have me, Doc. That's the only thing I can do. I'm poor as Job's turkey, you know." She smiled as she tossed her head.

Mandie's heart thumped loudly. *Marry— another man—soon as my father is gone*, she was thinking.

"Well, I suppose so. You could never make it

on your own here with two girls and no man around. I certainly wish I could have saved Jim, Etta. He was a fine man. He'll be hard to replace."

Mandie jumped up and ran out the back door. Joe came closely on her heels. She had tears in her eyes and didn't want Joe to see. He followed her as she raced up the mountain road to the cemetery where her father was buried and fell on her knees beside his grave, weeping uncontrollably.

"Mandie!" was all Joe said as he caught up with her, but she understood.

Finally she rose and wiped her tears on her apron. Joe held her small white hand.

"Just wait, Mandie. One day you and I will grow up and I will see that you are taken care of."

"That's a long time, Joe. Things may get worse."

"But I'll be around to help in the meantime," he assured her.

Joe came to the Shaw house more frequently after that and went with Mandie to put wild flowers on her father's grave. It was always a silent affair, neither speaking until they were back down the rough road.

Only one month after Jim Shaw had been laid to rest, Etta Shaw and Zach Hughes went into town together and came back to say they were married, and he moved into their house.

Mandie had seen him around a lot. He belonged to the same church and he was always offering to bring supplies from the store for them, or take them somewhere. He had never paid much attention to Mandie, but evidently he had been doing a lot of thinking and she was shocked when she was told what was planned for her.

They were sitting around the supper table on Friday night, two weeks after the wedding, when it happened.

"Well, Amanda," began Etta, clearing her throat. "We're a-fixin' to send you to live with the Brysons over yonder at Almond Station. They have a new baby and need some help."

"Mama!" was all she could say.

"Now, no argument! It ain't but two hoots and a holler away. We can't make a livin' here as 'tis and you'll just be one less mouth to feed. They'll give you a better home than we got here and plenty to eat," Etta told her.

"But, Mama—"

"Now, Amanda," Zach Hughes cut in. "We have already made the arrangements. They'll be here atter you tomarra morning so git your thangs together tonight."

Mandie, knowing she was beaten, fled from the table and went outside to sit in the dark under the chestnut trees. Snowball followed her and spread himself out across her feet.

She wished with all her might that Uncle Ned would come to see her. He had promised to watch over her and he had shown up at least once a week since her father had died. But he had already been there on Wednesday night and she didn't have much hope.

"Please, God, help me!" she pleaded, her face turned toward the moonlit sky. "Even if you don't love me anymore, won't you please help me?"

"Papoose need help. Me help." She couldn't believe her eyes when Uncle Ned stepped out from behind the tree in front of her and came forward. "Me help Papoose."

"Uncle Ned, how did you know? I didn't expect you again this week."

The old man sat down on the uncovered roots of the tree. "I know things. I hear things. I walk, no sound. I watch Papoose. Sit. Pow-wow. Tell trouble."

She sat down next to the old man and put her head against his deerskin jacket. She repeated what her mother and Zach had just told her.

"I know. I listen to talk. So, I come back." He put an arm around the child.

"But what can I do, Uncle Ned?"

"Papoose must go. Uncle Ned watch over her at new house. I promise Jim Shaw. I keep promise."

"I wish you were really my uncle." She smiled wistfully at the old Indian. "Then I could go live with you. You said I'm part Cherokee. Couldn't I just go home with you, Uncle Ned, please?"

"No, Papoose must get book learning. Jim Shaw say, you must go to school. When Papoose big squaw, then Papoose live with Cherokees."

"Amanda! Amanda!" Etta was calling from the back door. "Where're you at? Git back in this house and rid up these dishes!"

The old man quickly rose. "I go now. I watch Papoose new house. Better squaw not see me. I come again—full moon." He kissed the top of her head and silently disappeared into the darkness.

"Amanda!" Etta still yelled for her.

She walked slowly back to the house, the house where she had so many memories of her father, the house her father had built, now taken over by another man. She would leave because she would be forced to go, but she would come back someday. She would return to her father's house.

Before the first streak of light was in the sky the next morning, Mandie quietly rose, dressed, and hurried up the mountainside to her father's grave. Snowball bounced along before her.

She hurried, stumbling over the rough rocks, because she knew her mother would be looking for her. The weather was warmer now, but it was still chilly early in the morning. She held up her long skirt to keep it from getting wet in the early morning dew, and then seeing Indian Paintbrush blooming along the way, she quickly let go of her skirt and picked a handful of the bright flowers and ran on. Out of breath, she dropped on her knees by her father's grave and made a hole with a stick to plant the tiny bunch of flowers.

She sat back and folded her hands under her chin as she looked toward the sky. "Dear God, what time I am afraid I will put my trust in thee. I don't know what I did to cause you to take my daddy. I don't understand it, but I still love you."

Rising, she fought back the tears and ran back down the dirt road. She saw Mr. and Mrs. Bryson arriving in their buggy as she hastily ran in the back door and was confronted by her mother.

"Where've you been? Why, your skirt's all wet." Etta bent to touch the fabric. "I hear the Brysons now, so you'd better git your grits there in a hurry if you want any breakfast."

Etta went on into the front room where Mandie could hear her greeting the visitors. She slid into a chair and spooned out grits into her plate. She ate quickly, without saying a word to Snowball, as she fed him beneath the table. It was all she could do to keep from choking on the food. She was so fearful of what lay ahead for her. She had never spent a night away from home in her life and now she was being sent away to live with strangers.

Etta stuck her head through the doorway, "Git a move on, Amanda. They're in a hurry."

She jumped up, snatched Snowball up in her arms, and turned to face her mother defiantly. "I'm taking Snowball with me!"

"Well, take him. Be one less cat around here. Now come in here and meet the people you're goin' to live with."

Etta pushed her forward into the front room. A very fat young woman, evidently dressed in her Sunday-go-to-meeting clothes, sat near the door and a short, thin man stood nearby talking to Zach.

"My, my, she's an awful little thing," the woman exclaimed. "Is she big enough to be any good around the house?" The man silently turned to listen and look.

"Course she is. She's eleven year old atter all. Be twelve next week," Etta told the woman. "Just the age for you to train her the way you want."

Etta gave the girl another shove. "Now git your things, Amanda."

Mandie climbed the ladder and blindly crammed her few belongings into the flour sack her mother had given her. She picked up Snowball and went back downstairs. The Brysons were in a big hurry to get going.

Etta attempted to put an arm around the child. "Now you be a good girl. And remember we still love you."

Amanda tore loose, fighting the tears and the hatred she felt at that moment and ran into the yard, the Brysons following. She did not look back as they rode off until she knew her mother would be gone from the yard. Then she wiped her eyes and took one long, last look at her father's house.

*"He leadeth me
beside the still waters—"*

Chapter 3 / The Secret Journey

Sarah Bryson was the same age as Mandie, and at first Mandie thought she had found a friend. But soon she learned that Sarah was doing things she shouldn't and blaming them on Mandie, telling lies and getting her into trouble. And the Brysons always believed their daughter. Mandie was punished with a hickory switch on her legs, which she had never experienced in her life. Her father had never allowed it. Mandie was desperately afraid of the Brysons and no matter what she did, she could not please them with anything.

The new baby was an adorable little boy named Andrew and Mandie loved him immediately. But he was not her only duty. She had to help hoe corn and bring in the cows. And with a sinking heart, she learned she would not be allowed to attend school.

Furthermore, she had to stay home and watch Andrew while the Brysons went to church on Sunday!

Preacher DeHart came to preach on the first and third Sundays every month at the Brysons' church. The other Sundays he was at Maple Springs, the church Mandie belonged to back home. When he learned that the girl was living with the Brysons and was not allowed to come to church he came to see her.

"Remember the Sabbath Day to keep it holy, Amanda, even though you have to tend to the baby and can't go to church," he told her, as they sat in the Brysons' kitchen on Sunday afternoon after dinner. "You mustn't do anything to sin on the Lord's Day."

Mandie, always frightened by the big man's loud words, meekly said nothing, but, "Yes, sir, yes, sir."

She had known the preacher all her young life and she believed the bad things he said would happen to her if she did not live the right kind of life.

Her birthday came and went and no one even mentioned it. She wished the days by until the full moon when Uncle Ned had promised to visit her.

She sat in the swing under a tree in the backyard that night waiting for him, and when he made his stealthy appearance, she ran to him crying, pouring out her troubles.

"Don't cry, Papoose," he comforted her. "Cherokee think. I keep watch over Papoose. Cherokee think what to do."

The old Indian returned each week, but had not been able to come up with any solution to her problems. However, after Mandie had been living there for a few weeks, she happened to overhear a conversation which gave her some hope.

She was singing to the baby as she tried to rock him to sleep in his cradle in the room she shared with him. Mr. and Mrs. Bryson were in the next room and did not know the door was open.

"What are we going to do with that girl? She just can't do nothing right. We're gonna hafta git shed of her," Mrs. Bryson was speaking shrilly.

"Looks like Jim Shaw's brother over in Franklin would take care of her," Mr. Bryson replied.

"You know there's been hard feelings between Jim and John Shaw ever since Jim married—"

"That don't make no difference," Mr. Bryson interrupted. "This girl is the old man's niece and he ought to be responsible for her. He's got the money to support her."

"Well, I'm sure he knew Jim died and he never went near them." Mrs. Bryson changed the subject. "I think we orta git Dr. Woodard to look Andrew over. He's been lookin' mighty peaked lately."

"Seems all right to me, but I'll send word tomorrow if you want," her husband promised.

Mandie had stopped rocking the cradle when she heard the name and location of her father's brother. She would find him herself. And of all things—they were going to have Dr. Woodard come to see Andrew! That meant she could get a

36

message to Joe. Maybe things weren't so hopeless
after all. She didn't want to lose touch with Joe. He
was her only connection with her father's house.
Joe would be seeing her sister at school and would
know what was going on.

Andrew had finally dropped off to sleep. She
picked up an old catalogue lying nearby and tore
off a corner of a page that didn't have much print-
ing. She quickly found a pencil in her bag of per-
sonal belongings and wrote a message. "Going to
Franklin to live with Daddy's brother, John. Terrible
place here."

Dr. Woodard came two days later and Mandie
was overjoyed to see the old man as he pulled up in
his buggy.

"And how are you, Amanda? Joe hasn't been
over to your ma's lately, but he says your sister is
mean as ever." He laughed as he tweaked her long,
blonde braid. "You all right?"

"I'm fine, Dr. Woodard," she said, watching for
the Brysons as she followed the doctor into the
house. "Please give this to Joe for me," she whispered, pulling the folded piece of paper out of her
apron pocket and giving it to him. "Please don't tell
anyone."

Dr. Woodard winked at her and put the paper
in his vest pocket. "Be glad to, Amanda. Now I have
to see the baby."

It was full moon that night and the old Indian
showed up after suppertime. Mandie had rocked
Andrew to sleep and was sitting in the yard when he
appeared out of the trees. She got up and ran to him.

They sat down on the tree stump near the big black washpot hanging on its fork, with the two washtubs on a nearby bench shielding them from view.

"I have news, Uncle Ned," Mandie told him. "I overheard Mr. and Mrs Bryson talking about me. They said my Uncle John lives in Franklin. I have no idea which way that is. I need Cherokee help to get there, because I am going to live with him."

A big smile broke across the old man's face. "I glad. I am. Papoose go to uncle. No more trouble. Cherokee help. Find way. Bring food." He was almost as excited as the girl.

"When, Uncle Ned? I need to go as soon as possible. These people here don't like me and I'm afraid they might send me somewhere else."

"Next moon, I come back. I go now. Find way. Make plans with Cherokee. Must hurry." He rose.

"Thank you, Uncle Ned. Thank all of your people, or I should say, my people. They are my people, too, if they were my daddy's people."

"Yes, you Cherokee papoose. You go live with real uncle. Go to book school," he told her.

She wiped a tear of joy from her eyes, as he silently stole away into the darkness. "Thank you, dear God, thank you," she whispered as she looked up at the sky full of twinkling stars.

Doctor Woodard returned two days later to check on Andrew and he brought an answer to Mandie's message to Joe.

"I'm getting to be a regular mailman," he

laughed, as he tucked a small piece of paper into Mandie's apron pocket when she followed him out to his buggy. She gave his big hand a quick squeeze and ran away to the outhouse where she could read the note in privacy.

"My father takes me to Franklin with him some-times. Happy that you are going there. I will see you on my next visit there with my father—soon, I hope. Joe."

Mandie smiled to herself as she thought about the boy and his concern for her. It would be nice to see him again.

At the change of the moon, true to his word, Uncle Ned silently waited for Mandie in the dark-ness of the trees in the backyard. When Andrew was asleep, she quietly slipped out the back door and found him there.

"Franklin long moon away. We come, squaw and braves, to take Papoose. When moon rises three times we come here."

"Three days?" she asked.

He nodded.

"I will wait for you right here. Oh, I'm so—"

At that instant the back door opened and Sarah was calling to her as she came out into the yard. "Amanda, are you out there?" Sarah came into view and stopped. "Why, Amanda, who are you talking to out there?" She screamed as she came closer. "An Indian!" She turned to flee back to the house. Uncle Ned ran quickly away.

Mandie followed Sarah, running and calling, "It's all right, Sarah."

Mrs. Bryson appeared in the doorway. "What is going on?"

Sarah ran to her, clutching her long skirts. "An Indian! Amanda was talking to an Indian!"

"What!" Mrs. Bryson was shocked.

"It's all right. That was Uncle Ned. He was my daddy's friend," Mandie tried to explain.

"Your daddy's friend? An Indian?" Mrs. Bryson was white with fright as she turned back into the house.

"My daddy had lots of friends, all kinds," Mandie added.

"I never heard of Indian friends. What was he doing here?" The woman was furious now.

"He just keeps in touch with me. He promised my daddy he would," Mandie tried to reassure her.

"Keeps in touch with you?" Mrs. Bryson was still unsettled. "Now you listen here, young lady. Don't you dare let that Indian come back here again. Why, I'll have my husband shoot him! He'll steal us blind!"

"Oh, no, Mrs. Bryson!" Mandie broke into tears.

"Well, I'd better not catch him here again." She was very determined.

"You won't, Mrs. Bryson. I promise," she told her, silently thanking God that Uncle Ned was not to return again until he came after her. Then she would slip out and the Brysons would not see him.

The next three days dragged and it seemed as though the Brysons were meaner than usual to Mandie. They couldn't stop warning her about the old Indian. She tried her best to be patient and made her plans for the night when she would leave.

Andrew was more fretful than usual and she had a hard time getting him to go to sleep the night Uncle Ned was to return. She was almost sick with worry, fearing Uncle Ned would come with his friends and one of the Brysons would see them before she would be able to warn them.

At last the baby grew quiet and Mandie hastily gathered up her few belongings and crammed them into the same flour sack she had brought from home. Bending to kiss the chubby cheek of the sleeping infant and to scoop up Snowball in her arms, she picked up her bag and slipped outside into the warm summer darkness.

As soon as she had reached the shadows of the trees she saw Mr. Bryson come out the back door and settle down on the steps with his pipe. Her heart fluttered as she thought of the consequences should he catch the Indians there. She knew there was a pond nearby that was out of sight of the house and the Indians would probably pass it on their way. She hastened to the pond to intercept them.

The water seemed black and dangerous in the darkness, but Mandie sat down on a fallen log nearby to wait. After walking around in circles before deciding to curl up and sleep, Snowball softly purred in her lap.

Uncle Ned saw her first. He came quietly to stand at her side.

"Papoose, why you wait here?" he asked.

"Oh, Uncle Ned! I was afraid the Brysons would see you. They threatened to shoot you if you came back!" She stood up, catching Snowball as he fell. "Did the others come? Are we ready to go to Franklin?"

"Yes, Papoose. Come," he said and led the way back past the pond. There an old Indian squaw and two young braves waited for them.

Mandie ran to the old woman and hugged her tightly. It was so good to hug someone who cared for her. At that moment, a distant yell filled the air.

"Amanda! Amanda! Where are you, Amanda?"

The girl turned to Uncle Ned. "Quick! Let's go! That's Mrs. Bryson looking for me!"

The group ran through the cornfield, up the slope on the other side of the pond, and were soon hidden from the moonlight in the dark woods. Uncle Ned led the way and the two braves brought up the rear.

The old woman took Mandie's bag, threw it across her shoulder with her own bag, and grasped the girl's hand tightly as she hurried along.

Snowball stiffened in Mandie's arms, frightened because of the speed at which they were traveling. He didn't scratch the girl, but merely sank his claws into the shoulder of her dress and didn't move.

They did not slacken their pace until they reached the Nantahala River. There Uncle Ned stopped them.

"We cross here." He pointed to a narrow place

in the river where the rocks rose in the moonlight on the water. There was a footlog extending from side to side. "Then pass through Charley Gap. Papoose must not be seen there."

"Charley Gap? We're going right by my father's house?" Mandie questioned, her heart pounding.

"Yes. Big trouble if Papoose seen," Uncle Ned cautioned her. "We rest now." He sat down on a boulder nearby.

The two braves drifted, one on each side, and likewise sat down some distance away. Mandie dropped gratefully to the ground. Her feet hurt and her legs were tired. It seemed hours and hours since they had left the Brysons' land, and she was also sleepy and hungry.

There was the clanging of church bells in the distance and Mandie knew, with a sinking heart, that the Brysons must have sounded an alarm when they discovered her missing.

"The bells, Uncle Ned. They are probably getting a search party together."

"Don't worry, Papoose. They not find us," he told the girl. "Now we eat."

The Indian squaw brought forth meat and dark bread from her bag and held it out to the girl. Mandie thankfully took it and turned to the old man.

"She doesn't speak English, does she?" she asked.

"No. She know Indian talk. She good squaw. Name Morning Star."

Mandie turned back to the squaw. "Thank you, Morning Star."

The old woman smiled and bit into her own ration of food.

"Uncle Ned, does each Indian carry his own food? You have yours, and the other two men—do they have theirs?"

"Yes. We bring meat. Long way to Franklin."

When they had finished eating, Uncle Ned urged them on. "We go in dark. Sleep when sun shines. No one see."

The ringing of the church bells grew dimmer and then could no longer be heard as they made their way across the Nantahala River, went down Buckner Branch, and crossed the Tomahawk Trail. They had to stop often for Mandie to catch her breath. It was all up and down hill and through thick underbrush, and the rough rocks hurt her feet.

A long time later they approached Mandie's father's land. Uncle Ned halted the group.

"Careful. Follow me." He indicated that they were to swing out in a circle away from the house.

Mandie kept her eyes wide open, staring toward the darkened house and outbuildings. Evidently everyone was asleep at this hour. She almost wished she could run right past her mother and let her know that she had defied her and had run away from the Brysons. But she obeyed the old Indian, knowing she would be stopped if some of her people did see her.

She came to a sudden halt at the nearest point to the house, gazed at the log cabin with tears in her eyes, and then furiously ran ahead of the squaw in the direction Uncle Ned was taking.

She thought of her father's grave up the mountainside and wished she could visit it, but she knew it was out of their way. She would have to wait until someday in the future.

She would come back someday. She knew she would.

Her tired feet carried her off her father's land and on toward Franklin.

"He restoreth my soul—"

Chapter 4 / The Mansion

The first streaks of dawn were lighting up the sky when Uncle Ned finally stopped the group to sleep. They had just crossed Wiggins Creek when they finally sat down to rest.

Mandie flopped down on the grass. "Guess I'm plumb tuckered out." She laughed wearily.

Morning Star quickly gathered branches and made a bed for her to lie on, hidden under the trees. The girl used her shawl for a blanket, knowing when the sun came up it would be warm again.

She was so excited she couldn't sleep, but the fatigue overcame the excitement and she dropped off to dream.

The sound of shooting woke her. She sat up quickly and almost smashed Snowball, asleep by her side. For a minute she couldn't remember where she was. Then the old squaw put an arm around her and she relaxed. She could see Uncle Ned standing near the creek. He came to her. She could tell by his shadow that the sun was fast moving into the west. She must have slept all day.

"Braves go see where gun shoot," he told her. "They come, we go."

At that moment there was the sound of voices in the trees nearby.

"Well, I reckon we done searched fur enough. That girl couldn't 'a got no futher than this," a man's voice came to them.

Uncle Ned quickly whisked Mandie behind a laurel tree and he and the squaw slipped behind the rhododendron bushes nearby.

"Yeh, let's go see what's goin' on up yonder. Must be Jed's search party," another male voice replied.

Two men came into view. They were carrying rifles and stomping the underbrush beneath their feet. One was a tall man with a white beard and the other was a short, fat man who was spitting tobacco juice as he went. Mandie peeped around the tree, but she did not recognize either one. She realized they must be looking for her. They paused while the tall man lit his pipe.

"Don't much blame that youngun fer not wantin' to stay at that Bryson house. Hear tell that female is a tiger," the tall one was saying.

"Yep, I hear tell they can't nobody please her. But I shore would like to find that youngun 'fore the wildcats git her. I wouldn't want to take her back to the Brysons, but I wouldn't want her to git lost on this mountain either," the short one said. "I knew her pa. Good man, he was." They walked on, out of hearing, and were soon lost from sight in the tall underbrush.

The squaw went to Mandie and put her arm around her. Uncle Ned followed.

"Be not afraid, Papoose. We go to Franklin. White men not stop Indians," he reassured the girl.

"I know. I know how smart the Indians are. I know you will get me to my uncle's house in Franklin," she replied, grasping the old man's hand. "I'm not afraid. After all, I'm part Cherokee, too."

The two braves came silently up to the old man.

"White men carry guns; coming this way," the taller one said.

"Two passed here," Uncle Ned told them. "Looking for Papoose. We go." He pointed in the direction of Hightower Gap away from the way the two men had gone.

The group slipped quietly through the woods, resting only when Mandie was tired, and they finally reached the Little Tennessee River. They took long detours for safety's sake but followed the banks of the river most of the way. They came on through Burningtown and up the main road that ran through Franklin.

The sight before her was unbelievable to Mandie. All the houses were so close together and there were so many of them. Then there were all the

stores. They passed the livery stable. It was barely
dawn, but there was the sound of voices and
horses. She was speechless as she stared around
her.

"John Shaw that way." Uncle Ned pointed
down the long main road. "Take Papoose to house.
White man must not see Indian."

He halted in front of an immense white house
with a huge yard covered with green grass, flowers,
and shrubs, and a small summerhouse at one side.
A white picket fence enclosed the yard and a hitching post with a stepping-stone was at the gate.
Across the road was an old church with a cemetery.

Mandie stood in frozen awe at the monstrous
size of the house and the surrounding yard and gar-
dens. So this was Uncle John's mansion. It must
have twenty rooms, at least. She at once became
nervous and excited at the prospect of meeting her
father's brother. What if he didn't like her? What if
she had to go back to the Brysons? But then, she
would not think of such things, because she would
not go back to the Brysons under any circum-
stances. She would go live with Uncle Ned's tribe if
her uncle rejected her.

"Go, Papoose," Uncle Ned urged her. "I come
later. Love."

"And love to you, Uncle Ned and Morning
Star." She turned to hug the old Indian and the
squaw, and then quickly opened the gate and ran
up the steps to the front porch. She lifted a shaking

hand to knock on the front door.

She could not hear a sound inside. No one seemed to be at home. Her heart sank. She turned to look at the Indians who were half hidden by the shrubbery. Then she heard footsteps coming closer to the door. She looked up to see a big, tall man, barefooted and in workclothes, standing before her.

"Are you John Shaw?" she asked nervously.

"No, ma'am. He's not home." The man scratched his gray head as he stared at her.

"When will he be back? You see, I'm his niece, Amanda Shaw," she explained.

"Well, come in, miss." The man held the door open and Mandie turned to catch a glimpse of Uncle Ned's smiling face.

She entered a wide hallway and followed the man to a room on the right, which she decided must be the company parlor judging from the rich furnishings. She sat down on the edge of a soft armchair and deposited her bag on the floor by her side. Snowball escaped from her arms and went running off into the other part of the house.

"When will Uncle John be back?" she asked.

"Oh, he's gone to Europe. He's been gone since March. I'm the caretaker, Jason Bond." He was still standing as he explained.

"Oh, goodness, to Europe!" She was dismayed to have come all this way and then not find her uncle at home. "What will I do?"

"Where're you from, miss?"

"I lived with my daddy, Jim Shaw, and my mother over at Charley Gap in Swain County until my daddy died in April and my mother got married again. Then they sent me away to live with some awful people at Almond Station and I ran away." She told the man the truth, knowing her uncle would have to know. "I—I don't have anywhere to live."

"Oh, well, plenty of room here. He oughta be back any day now. Come on, I'll find you a room." He picked up her bag and led the way up a long flight of stairs to the second floor, and then down a long hall and opened the door to a room furnished with blue and gold. Mandie stared in delight. Never had she seen such an elegant room.

"How about this one?" Jason Bond was asking as she stood there.

"Oh, it's beautiful! It's wonderful!" She stood in the middle of the room, gazing about.

"I'll get Liza to bring you some fresh water for your pitcher over there, and some breakfast if you ain't et yet."

"Oh, I am hungry," she said. "In fact, I'm starving!" She laughed.

"Well, we'll fix that." Jason Bond went out the door and she removed her wrinkled bonnet, tossed it on the bed and sat down in a big, soft chair. She had a strange feeling that she must be in the wrong house. How could her uncle have so much when her father had had so little?

An enormous old black woman knocked and

then came on in with a tray of food, followed by a young black girl with a bucket of water.

"I'm Lou, Aunt Lou, they call me, my child. I keeps this house together." She set the tray on a table nearby and stood before Mandie. "Now, what might be your name?"

"Amanda Shaw, Aunt Lou. My daddy was Jim Shaw, John's brother." She lifted the cloth covering the food and exclaimed, "Oh, thank you, Aunt Lou. I'll eat every bite; I'm so hungry."

"Well, you'd better had if you gonna stay around here. Now this here's Liza. She'll be lookin' after you whiles you here." She beckoned to the young girl who still stood behind her. Liza came forward and poured the water into the pitcher on the washstand.

"Guess you'd better wash that dirty face 'fore you eat." Aunt Lou smiled at her. "Liza, you comb that pretty hair for my child. But let her eat first."

Aunt Lou left the room and Mandie went to wash her face in the bowl of water.

"I be back later, Miss Amanda," Liza told her. "You want anything, all you has to do is pull that cord over there."

"Pull that cord?" Mandie asked, looking to where Liza was pointing toward the drapery beside the bed.

Liza laughed and danced around the room. "That makes a bell ring down at the other end where I hear it and I knows you calling me." She danced on out the door, laughing.

Snowball came running into the room and jumped up into Amanda's lap as she sat down to eat.

"You just wait, Snowball. You have to eat on the floor. Here," she said, putting him down and giving him some milk in a saucer that had been on her tray. She added a bit of bacon. "Now you eat it all up because we're going to take a nap."

True to her word, she, with Snowball's help, ate every bite of the food and then, pulling down the silky bedspread, she flopped onto the big soft bed and fell fast asleep with the kitten curled up beside her.

At noontime Liza came to call the girl to dinner and had to wake her.

"Time to eat, Miss Amanda," Liza said, shaking the girl.

Mandie sat up rubbing her eyes. "Eat? I just ate. Oh, goodness, what time is it?" Snowball rose and stretched.

"It's time to eat again. Wash your face and I'll comb that hair," Liza told her.

The black girl quickly unbraided Mandie's hair, combed out the many tangles and then braided it again.

"I think I'll wash your hair later," Liza suggested.

"Oh, yes, it is dirty," Mandie agreed, remembering the bed of twigs she had slept on and the many miles she had walked through briars, dusty roads and river water.

"Later," Liza said. "Now you just follow me. I'll

show you where the food be."

They went back down the long, carpeted hall, down the elaborate staircase and through another long hall into the most beautiful room Mandie had ever seen. A huge crystal chandelier hung over an enormous dining table covered with a crocheted tablecloth and set with one place at the end for her. Silver candelabra stood at intervals along the table. A whole wall was covered by a tapestry of peacocks and flowers. The opposite side of the room had long French doors opening onto a terrace. Mandie stopped to gaze about the room.

"Here, missy, down to this end," Liza beckoned to her as she pulled out a chair with a velvet seat. "You set right here and I bring on the food."

Mandie, still speechless, walked to the chair and sat down. Then she turned quickly as the girl turned to leave the room. "What do you have to eat?"

"Anything you want, missy. Ham, chicken, sweet potatoes, green beans, turnip salat, cornpone, biscuits, honey, preserves, anything you want. Now what must I bring you?" Liza waited.

"You mean you have all those things already cooked? All for one meal?"

"Well, missy, all us servants have to eat too, and there's two more 'sides me and Lou. There's Jenny, the cook, and there's Abraham, the yard man, what lives in the house in the backyard. Lou, she's the boss," Liza went on. "So we just cook everything at one time. That's the way Mr. Shaw tells us to do. Want me to bring you some of everything?" Liza grinned.

"Oh, no, I couldn't possibly eat so much. Just a small piece of ham, a spoonful of green beans, a huge sweet potato, a big piece of cornbread, and milk," Mandie told her. "My uncle must be an awfully rich man if he has all that for one meal."

"Oh, he is, missy. Richest man this side of Richmond, they say. So much money he'll never spend it all. And no one to leave it to—except—"

Aunt Lou came through the door at that moment.

"Liza, git a move on here. Take that cat there and feed it and git this child something to eat. And no more of that gossip, you hear?"

Without a word, Liza took Snowball and quickly left the room.

"And how is my child feeling after her nap?" Aunt Lou put her arm around Mandie's shoulders.

"Fine, Aunt Lou. Liza says my uncle is unusually rich; it that so?"

"I don't knows about it being unusual, but he shore is rich. Liza ain't got no business meddling in his affairs like that, though."

"She wasn't meddling, Aunt Lou. I asked her. You see, my daddy was never rich."

"Many's a good man that don't git rich."

"You see, you can tell by my clothes that I am not rich. I don't have any pretty, fancy dresses and bonnets." Mandie smoothed her dark gray frock.

"Well, that's one thing we's can fix, my child.

We's got a sewing room here that's just plumb spang full of pritty cloth. We'll just make you up some new clothes," Aunt Lou was telling her as Liza came back into the room carrying a silver tray loaded with dishes and the smell of hot food. "Now you just eat up, my child, and Liza can bring you 'round to the sewing room when you git done. I'll see what we can whip up."

"Thank you, Aunt Lou. I'll hurry," Mandie assured her, as she picked up her fork. The black woman left the room. "Don't go away, Liza. I'll be finished in a minute."

"I has to go eat, too, but I'll be right back. Just pull that little cord over there by the window if you want me. It'll ring in the kitchen," Liza told her.

"You haven't eaten yet? I thought I was the only one left to eat dinner," Mandie told her. "Go get your food and come sit right here." She pushed out a chair next to her with her foot.

Liza laughed. "You don't understand, missy. I'se a servant. Us servants has our own table in the kitchen."

"But I'm the only one at this big table. Can't you come and eat with me?"

"Nope, can't," Liza replied. "Nobody exceptin' Mr. Bond and Mr. Shaw eats at that table, and you, of course, 'cause you'se kin."

"Where is Mr. Bond?"

"He et early 'cause he had to go off and tend to some bidness," the dark girl told her. "Now you eat up. I'll go eat and then I'll be back."

Liza laughed and danced out through the door. Mandie, famished as she was, hurriedly ate the rich food in anticipation of getting a new dress made for her—a brand new dress made just for her—one that nobody had ever worn.

When Liza took her to the sewing room, Mandie was again amazed with the wonders of her uncle's house. It looked like a store. Fine materials, laces, ribbons, buttons of every color, were everywhere about the room. Aunt Lou, who was also the seamstress for the household, was waiting for her.

"You just pick out what you want and we make it," the old woman told her.

Mandie immediately spied a roll of pale blue silk in the pile. She stroked the soft material with her fingertips.

"This one, please," the girl murmured shyly. "I've never had a light-colored dress in my life."

"And a bonnet to match." Aunt Lou smiled at her. "We'll just put lots of trimming on it—lace, ribbons, and sech. We'll make a real baby doll out of you, that's what we'll do."

Mandie spent the afternoon in the room while Aunt Lou pinned, measured, and cut material. She just couldn't believe it would all turn into a dress just for her. When Aunt Lou was ready to sew, Liza came to tell Mandie she had a visitor in the parlor.

"Miss Polly, that lives in that big house next-door, she's come to see you, missy," Liza said. "She waiting in the parlor for you."

"In the parlor? I don't even know where the

parlor is," Mandie laughed bewilderedly. "I've never seen such a big house in my life."

"Right this way." Liza led her. "Down this hall and on down these steps and it's the big double door on the left, next to the front door. 'Member the room where you first came in?"

"I remember the room, but I didn't remember the way. Thank you, Liza." Mandie went on through the double door and there stood a girl about her own size in front of the sofa.

She had long, dark hair and eyes as dark as chinquapins. She smiled and came forward.

"My name's Polly Cornwallis. I live next door, and Mr. Shaw's cook told our cook that Mr. Shaw's niece had come to visit, and so I came over." She rolled off this long speech without taking a breath.

"I'm glad you live next door," Mandie told her. "Sit down."

They sat on the sofa.

"My name is Amanda Shaw. My uncle is gone off to Europe and I'm here alone, so I'm glad you came."

They were friends at once and before they realized it, Liza was telling them supper was ready. Polly had to go home, but promised to come back the next day and bring her schoolbooks. But the next day brought more than Polly and her schoolbooks for Mandie.

"He leadeth me in the paths of righteousness for his name's sake—"

Chapter 5 / The Secret Tunnel

Early the next morning, Jason Bond answered a knock at the front door. He found a messenger there from John Shaw's lawyer's office in Asheville.

"Mr. Wilson sent you this letter, Mr. Bond," the young boy told him.

Mr. Bond took the letter, withdrew a paper from the envelope, and stood there reading.

"What's this? What's this?" Jason Bond was plainly shocked. "Come on in, my boy. I'll get the cook to give you something to eat. I'll have to send an answer back."

He took the boy to the kitchen and left him there with Jenny. Then he hurried to his room and wrote a note. Hearing Mandie singing in her room, he knew she was up, and knocked on her door.

"I see you're up bright and early. Come on

downstairs. I have something to tell you." He led the way down to the dining room and yelled through the door to Jenny.

"Send Liza in here with something to eat," he said and went back to sit down by the girl at the table.

"What's wrong, Mr. Jason?" Mandie asked him. She could sense he was disturbed about something.

"Well, it's like this," he began, as Liza brought in the coffee and poured it. He waited until she left the room. "I have a letter here from your uncle's lawyer."

"You do?" Mandie leaned forward.

"Yes, but I'm afraid it's bad news. He says—he says your uncle has—died in Europe and—"

"Died! Oh, no!" she gasped and brought her hand to her mouth. "Please, God, not my Uncle John, too!"

"I'm sorry," Mr. Bond said. "I couldn't think of any way to tell you. The letter says he was buried over there and—"

"When, Mr. Jason?"

"A few weeks ago. It took a long time for word to reach his lawyer and then his lawyer had to let us know," the old man told her.

"Oh, Uncle John, now what will I do?" she sobbed.

Mr. Bond held her hand and tried to comfort her. "Don't worry about what you're going to do. You're going to stay right here. I'm sending a note back to the lawyer, telling him you are here and you are going to stay here until the will is found."

"The will?" she asked.

"Yeh, until the will is found. Lawyer Wilson drew up a will for your uncle last year, but he says in this letter he believes your uncle made another one since then. At any rate, he thinks the will must be in his papers here in the house somewhere, so we'll have to look for it."

"What good is the will if Uncle John is dead?" she asked.

"Don't you know what a will is? It's a paper, a legal paper, stating who is to receive what of the inheritance when a person dies. Your uncle had lots of money and property and someone will get all that, depending on who is mentioned in his will," Mr. Jason told her. "There's a possibility you will be mentioned in his will as a legal heir."

"An heir?"

"Yes, that's the person who gets whatever is left to him by the person who dies."

"But he never even saw me that I know of. He might not have even known that I was born."

"Maybe, maybe not. Anyway, he knew he had a brother, who was your father; and since your father is dead, if he willed anything to him, then you would get it instead."

Mandie finally understood most of what Mr. Bond was telling her, and she became anxious to find the will. She also wanted to talk to someone her own age.

"May I invite Polly to spend the night with me, Mr. Bond?"

"Of course, but her mother will have to agree, you know."

So when Polly came over and heard the news, she returned home to tell her mother and came back to tell Mandie that her mother would come to call later in the afternoon.

Mrs. Cornwallis, a young widow, was very expensively dressed; her clothes were beautiful. Mandie was a little unsure of herself in the presence of such a lady.

"My dear, such a shock for you. And just the day after you got here, too. You must come over to our house and stay until things are settled," Mrs. Cornwallis told her.

"Thank you, Mrs. Cornwallis, but I can't leave. I have to help Mr. Jason look for Uncle John's will," Mandie said. "And I would like Polly to spend the night with me, if you would let her."

"Yes, yes, of course, dear," Polly's mother agreed. "But, doesn't anyone know where John Shaw kept his will?"

"No, not even his lawyer. He says it must be somewhere here in the house, so we have to find it."

"Mandie, can I help you look?" Polly put in.

"That's why I wanted you to spend the night," Mandie replied.

Mrs. Cornwallis rose to go. "Polly can spend the night, dear; but please get some sleep, girls." She laughed as she left.

"Will you have to go home now because your uncle died? I sure hope not," Polly said.

"Oh, no, Mr. Jason said I was to stay here until the will is found; and we're going to find it ourselves. Come on! We'll start right now."

The two girls left Polly's nightclothes in Mandie's room and then in whispers decided to take candles and go up to the third floor. Mandie had not yet been to the third floor of the house, and was anxious to do a little exploring.

They found the door to the stairs, turned the knob and it opened. Silently they gazed up the dark steps, then slowly began their ascent on the creaking stairway. They reached a landing halfway up and stopped to open the window and push open the shutters to let in the light and fresh air before climbing the last flight.

"At last!" sighed Polly, as they reached yet another door at the top of the stairs.

Upon opening it, they found themselves in a long hallway. Holding their half-spent candles at arm's length, they cautiously followed the corridor to the only door they could see in the hall, at the left. Mandie, arriving first, pushed it open.

Before them was a huge, impressive bedroom furnished with two ornately carved four-poster beds. Each was covered with a white crocheted spread and draped with matching canopy curtains. There were two full-length mirrors with heavy wood frames to match the beds. Four tall windows were covered with sheer Priscillas.

Before the girls could take in more in the meager light, the canopy curtain moved slightly on one of the beds and they heard a strange noise. At the same time, a draft from somewhere snuffed out their candles. With this, the frightened girls ran down the hall in search of the stairway. Just as they reached it, the door slammed violently and when they grabbed for the doorknob they discovered there was none.

Mandie gasped and clung to Polly as the two raced down to the other end of the hall. In the darkness they both stumbled into the wall, pushing a hidden panel open which led to yet another descending stairway. Just when they were beginning to wonder if the stairs would end, they came to a short hallway. They could see no door, but more stairs led downward and they took the plunge hand in hand.

To continue the maze, they found another door, opened it and stumbled into a dark room, managing to cross it without bumping into any furniture. A second door in the room led to another stairway, at which point Mandie cried, "Where in the world are we?"

"Don't ask me," was Polly's bewildered reply.

At the end of another hall they came upon a locked door, but this time Polly discovered a large key dangling on a nail beside the door. With a trembling hand she inserted the key in the lock. Exhausted with suspense and fear she handed the key to Mandie and asked her to open the door. To the complete surprise of both the girls there were bushes and vines growing directly in front of them in the open doorway. They pushed through the shrubbery and exclaimed together, "We're in the woods!"

They could barely see the back of the house through all the trees.

"It was a secret tunnel, just like in the story-books!" cried Polly.

"It's amazing! I can hardly believe this is happening," added Mandie.

"Say, I'm getting awfully hungry," murmured Polly. "It must be close to dinnertime."

"Yeh, me too. Come on, let's run," Mandie called as she bounded toward the other side of the house.

Polly caught up with her. "Let's keep this *our* secret. Then we can explore it all over again."

"All right. We won't tell anyone where we've been," Mandie agreed. "But I sure would like to know what was behind that curtain on that bed. Ooh, it makes me shiver just to think of it!"

"I know," agreed Polly. "Let's get Mr. Bond to go up there with us and see what it is."

"That's a good idea. Come on. Let's hurry and eat dinner." Mandie once again broke into a run.

As they came in the back door Aunt Lou greeted them. "Land sakes! Where you all done been? Vittles bein' put on the table. Git a move on and git washed. Quick!" She shooed them on through the kitchen with a big grin, as they obeyed.

They washed, hurried to the dining room and slipped into their chairs just as Mr. Bond came in right behind them.

"Well, well, where have you two been for so long?" he asked.

"We've been looking for the will," Polly said, quickly.

"On the third floor," added Mandie, watching for his reaction.

"On the third floor, eh? Well, did you find anything up there?" He began slicing the ham.

"Yes," Polly said.

"But we don't know what it is," Mandie reminded her.

"Well, what's that supposed to mean? How did you find something if you don't know what it is?"

"We found a big bedroom with ghost-white curtains and spreads over two big four-poster beds on the third floor, with white curtains all over all the windows. It makes chills run down my spine!" Mandie exaggerated.

"Mine, too! It made a noise, Mr. Bond, and made the curtains move and then it blew out our lights," Polly told him.

"Well now, if you'll eat up, we'll just go back up there and see what it is."

They were soon finished and Mr. Bond went to get some matches and an oil lamp.

Mandie absentmindedly slipped her hand into her pocket. "I still have the key to that tunnel," she whispered.

"Listen, let's tell Mr. Bond about it—just him—nobody else?" begged Polly.

"All right, but not till we see what the ghost is," cautioned Mandie as Mr. Bond returned.

They followed the kind man up the stairs silently, darting glances all around. When they reached the landing where they had opened the window, he closed it, commenting that the draft might cause their lamp to go out. Arriving at the top of the stairs he opened the door into the center hall of the third floor.

"Land sakes! Gotta replace that knob," he said, as he noticed the other side of it was missing.

The girls followed more closely behind him.

"It was in that room," Mandie said, pointing to the door on the left.

"All right, we'll just see what's in there," the caretaker told them. He walked over to the bed and the curtains moved. And there was that noise again!

As he touched the curtain a bat flew out from behind it. The girls screamed and ran into the hall. After a long chase, Mr. Bond finally ran the bat out through the window in the hall and closed it again, leaving the shutters open to allow some light from outside.

"Come on back in now and see for yourselves, girls. It's gone," he assured them.

The two slowly entered the room, looked cautiously around and were satisfied.

"Mr. Jason, we found a secret tunnel today

right here in this house," Mandie blurted out.

"A secret tunnel?" the old man asked.

"Yes, come on! We'll show you!" Mandie fairly danced about.

"It goes into the woods," Polly said.

"I don't know anything about a secret tunnel in this house," Mr. Bond said.

The girls explained how they had found it. They led the way down the hall and searched for the loose panel. Instead, they found a door they hadn't seen before, which opened to a small room containing steps which led to the attic.

"Well, reckon that's it," Mr. Bond said. "We've looked everywhere and haven't found it yet. There's only one more door left and it's locked." He indicated a door near where they were standing.

"Oh, we missed that one," Mandie jumped.

"I've got the key I know what's in there," Mr. Bond said.

"Here," Mandie pulled the key from her pocket. "I have the key to the door at the other end of the tunnel. We can come in from that end."

"Too late tonight for such things," Mr. Bond said. "We'll try it tomorrow in the daylight."

"Well, if you have the key to this room, can we see what's in there?" Polly asked.

Mr. Bond took out his keys and fumbling through them came up at last with the key that unlocked the door. The girls stepped ahead of him into the room and looked around in surprise.

There were shelves on three sides of the room

filled with books. In front of a large stained-glass window was a huge desk with papers strewn about on it. All the shutters were open, letting in the moonlight from outside. On the opposite side of the room was a beautifully carved couch with big soft cushions. On the three sides with shelves there were wall sconces holding candles, as many as could possibly be placed between the rows of books.

Mandie noticed a smaller door in one corner which she tried to open and found locked. The caretaker had no key for it. She also noticed an ashtray with ashes in it on the desk and a pen in a bottle of ink.

"Wonder what your uncle used this room for—a private library?" Polly asked.

"He did his private book work up here," Mr. Bond told them. "None of the servants are allowed on the third floor."

"Do you know what's on the other side of that locked door, Mr. Jason?" Mandie wanted to know.

"Nope, can't say I remember ever seeing it before. Believe those curtains may have been pulled over it when I've been in here, and that's not been many times."

"Can we light the candles, Mr. Bond, so we can see how they look all burning at one time?" Polly begged.

Mr. Bond struck a match, lighted one candle, and the one on either side of it automatically burst into flame. He repeated this around the room.

"You see how close they are? That's what makes 'em all light up magic-like," the old man told them.

The room was brilliant, and Mandie's attention was drawn to a paper on top of the pile on the desk.

She picked it up and read aloud, " 'March 1st. Dear Brother Jim'—This is to my daddy!—'I am going on vacation to Europe for the summer and since one never knows what the future on a ship can hold, I would like to make peace with you while I can. I am an old man now, fifteen years older than you, you know, and I have no one to leave my belongings to, except you. I am taking the blame entirely for the disagreement between us all these years. I want you to know that Elizabeth is still in love with you, and she says she will never love anyone else. All that matters to me now is—' " Mandie looked up, puzzled. "That's all; it's unfinished. Who is Elizabeth?"

Mr. Bond took the paper and read it over again. "I'm afraid I have no idea who Elizabeth is."

"I wonder why it's not finished," Mandie mused.

"Might have been written over again on another piece of paper. See that ink blot?" He showed her a black smear of ink on the paper, which she had not noticed.

"You're right, Mr. Jason," Mandie's blue eyes filled with tears. "I hope my daddy received that letter before he—passed away."

"He probably did." Mr. Bond put the paper back on the desk and reached for a long rod.

"What's that?" Polly wanted to know.

"It's a snuffer, to put out all these confounded candles," he said, as he swung it around the room extinguishing each one as he went.

"Imagine doing this every day," Polly remarked.

"Yeh, and I'm glad I don't have to," he said.

Once in her room for the night, with only Polly for company, Mandie studied the paper again, which she had taken from the library. She was glad Polly's mother had agreed to let her stay with her until her uncle's missing will was found.

"I hope my daddy got this," she said again. "I have to find this Elizabeth who loved him."

"In the meantime, tomorrow we'll show Mr. Jason the tunnel," Polly reminded her. "What did you do with the key?"

"I put it on the bureau over there." Mandie pointed to it.

But, in the morning the key was gone. It was nowhere to be found.

"Yea, though I walk through the valley of the shadow of death, I will fear no evil—"

Chapter 6 / The Ghost

One morning, later that week, the two girls had wandered across the road through the cemetery, reading stone markers and commenting about the names, when they perceived someone knocking at John Shaw's front door.

They hurried across the road to find a tall young man with big hazel eyes, standing there with a black traveling bag in his hand.

He looked down at the girls, smiled, and asked, "Is this where Mr. John Shaw lived before he died abroad?"

"Yes, sir," Mandie told him. "I'm his niece, Amanda Shaw."

"You are?" he questioned her. "I'm his nephew. You live here?"

"Yes, come on in and sit down. I'll get Mr. Bond." She opened the door and met Mr. Bond in

71

the hallway. "Mr. Bond, this is Uncle John's nephew."

The old man quickly looked the young man over and said slowly, "Mr. John Shaw didn't have any nephews."

"Well, I'm Bayne Locke, his sister's son. And since I *am* his nephew, I have come to claim my part of his property," the young man told him.

"I said, Mr. Shaw did not have any nephews; in fact, no living relatives, except his brother, Jim, and his family and they live in Swain County," Jason Bond was emphatic.

"I am John Shaw's *nephew*," the stranger insisted, standing there in the hallway. "My mother died when I was born and I never have seen my uncle, but I'm sure I can claim at least part of what he owned. Where's his will?"

Mr. Bond looked puzzled, scratching his head thoughtfully. "To tell you the truth, we haven't found the will yet. But we have received word from his lawyer concerning the property—"

The young man interrupted, "I have as much right to stay here as anyone else until the will is found, if it *is* ever found." He plopped his bag on the floor.

"Oh, it'll be found all right," Mr. Bond told him.

"Well, until it is found, please show me my room. I've been traveling all the way from Richmond and I'm tired," Bayne Locke demanded.

"I suppose you can stay here tonight, but I'll have to have proof as to who you are," the old man said.

"I have it right here." Bayne pulled a paper from his inside pocket and handed it to Mr. Bond.

"All this says is that you are the son of Martha Shaw and Caro Locke. It does not prove you're John Shaw's nephew."

"Anybody that knows the Shaw family knows that he had a sister who died twenty-two years ago giving birth to a son in Richmond," Bayne told him.

Mr. Bond still stood there scratching his head. Mandie was left speechless with the matter. Then Polly suddenly looked from Bayne to Mandie and spoke up.

"Well, Mandie, you have a cousin!" she exclaimed.

"Well, sort of, I suppose I do," Mandie agreed. Then she turned to Mr. Bond. "I'll show my cousin to a room, Mr. Bond. Which room should I put him in?"

"Either one down the hall upstairs. I'll get Liza to go up and get things ready." Mr. Bond turned back down the hallway toward the kitchen.

The girls led the young man up the stairs, past Mr. Bond's room, to an unoccupied bedroom.

Mandie pushed open the door and peered into the room. It was well furnished with heavy furniture, red rugs and gold draperies.

"This will have to do," she said, standing aside for Bayne Locke to enter the room. "It's on the front of the house and won't get the afternoon sun."

"Fine, fine," Bayne muttered, throwing up the windows and opening the shutters.

Liza danced in with a broom and a dustmop.

"Shoo, shoo! You-alls just git out of the way now, so's I can git this place shuck up," the black girl ordered the girls.

Mandie turned back as she went out the door, followed by Polly.

"Dinner's at twelve o'clock on the button. Don't be late."

"Never been to dinner on time in my life, but I'll turn over a new leaf just for you," Bayne called back to her.

As the two girls sat in the swing on the front porch, Polly asked, "What are you going to do now? That man says he's your cousin, and he'll take what he came after, if you ask me."

"We'll see about that! Just leave him to me!" Mandie teased.

"But what can you do about it?" Polly wanted to know.

"Tonight's the night for Uncle Ned to come visit," Mandie said.

"Uncle Ned? Who's he?"

"He's the Indian who brought me here. Remember I told you?"

"Yeh, but so what? What can an Indian do about this Bayne Locke?"

"I'll ask Uncle Ned to get the Cherokees to check up on this so-called cousin. Uncle Ned has his own ways of finding out things."

The screen door opened and Aunt Lou stuck her head out. "Got that new dress done fuh you, my child."

Mandie quickly followed her back into the house with Polly close behind. The blue dress was finished and pressed and was hanging in the sewing room. Mandie could only stand and gasp. She had never owned such a garment in all her life.

"Well, don't just stand there, my child. We'se got to put it on to see if it fits." Aunt Lou smiled as she began to unbutton the dress Mandie was wearing.

The dress fit perfectly and Mandie turned and twirled in front of the long mirror with oh's and ah's and Polly admiring.

"It's beautiful, Aunt Lou." Mandie was tearful as she turned to hug the old woman tightly. "Thank you, Aunt Lou! Thank you!"

"It takes a pretty girl like you to make a dress pretty," Aunt Lou told her. "You look mighty fine, my child."

"Positively heavenly, Mandie," Polly agreed.

"Will you unbutton me now, Aunt Lou?" Mandie asked

"Unbutton you? What for? There's more acomin' from where that one came from. Now you just keep it on and enjoy it, my child." The old woman patted her on the head.

"More, Aunt Lou?"

"Sho' 'nuff. Next one will be ready 'fore you git that one dirty," Aunt Lou assured her. "Gonna be the lady of the house, you is. And you gotta look like the lady of the house—no more countrified looks. You'se a city girl now. Gotta dress like city folks."

"But, Aunt Lou, I hate to make so much work for you. You have other things to do, I know."

"Ain't just me working on these dresses. Got help from old Miz Burnette over on the hill, too."

"Mrs. Burnette makes my clothes too, Mandie," Polly told her. "Mother says she does the best work in town."

"Somebody has to pay her," Mandie said.

"Oh, never you mind about pay. Mr. Bond done arranged all that. Now git on 'bout your business. I'se got other things to do," Aunt Lou gave the two girls an affectionate shove out the door.

Thank you, dear God, Mandie whispered to herself. Thank you for all these nice things.

That night, when Mandie met Uncle Ned in the summerhouse nearby, she wore her new blue dress. The old Indian was happy when she told him about all the nice things that had happened to her, but he was greatly disturbed when he heard that her Uncle John had died and Bayne Locke had come to the house saying he was his nephew.

"Bayne Locke. You know where he come from?" he asked.

"He said he had come all the way from Richmond, Uncle Ned," Mandie told him. "I suppose he must have lived there before he came here."

"Cherokee go to Richmond. Find out. I know by next full moon," he promised.

"Thank you, Uncle Ned. I seem to ask you for so many things, but I don't have anyone else to ask," the girl said.

"No, no—is all right. You one of us. Cherokee keep watch over Papoose. I promise Jim Shaw. Anything you ask, I do," Ned reminded her. "You Cherokee, too."

"Isn't that wonderful, Uncle Ned? That I have such people, people who will always look out for me. Tell all the Cherokees I am grateful. I'm happy that I'm one of you and I long for the day when I can visit my people."

Not only was Mandie planning to check up on Bayne Locke, but Mr. Bond had immediately sent a messenger to Lawyer Wilson's office, requesting information concerning the young man.

Later that night when he thought everyone was sound asleep, Mr. Bond climbed the stairs to the third story in a determined effort to locate John Shaw's will and settle the matter once and for all as far as Bayne Locke was concerned.

John Shaw's library was directly over the room that Mandie and Polly occupied on the second floor and he tried to be very quiet, but despite his efforts, he stumbled into a chair in the darkness.

"Polly, did you hear that?" Mandie shook her sleeping friend.

"Yes," Polly said, sitting straight up in the bed.

"A ghost!" Mandie whispered.

"In Uncle John's library! Let's go see what it is," Polly said, jumping from the bed.

"This time of night?" Mandie was leery of such adventures.

"Ghosts only walk at night. Didn't you know

that?" Polly informed her. "I read a book about ghosts once. They can't do you any harm. So why be afraid? We're more powerful than they are. Want to go see what one really looks like?"

"Oh, Polly, you aren't afraid of anything, are you?" Mandie reached for her slippers. "Let's go, if you insist."

Polly led the way up the dark stairs while Mandie carried the oil lamp from her room. They crept along the hall and found the door open to Uncle John's library. As they cautiously peeped in, Mandie began to laugh.

"Some ghost that is!"

Mr. Bond turned at the sound of her voice. "Why, what are you two doing up this time of night?"

"We heard a noise, so we came up to see who it was," Polly answered. "We had kinda hoped it was a ghost."

"Well, I'm not a ghost," Mr. Bond chuckled. "But I'd advise you two to be quiet and not disturb the rest of the house. I don't want that Mr. Locke poking his nose in here."

"No, that wouldn't do," Mandie agreed. "He might find the will before we do. Can we do anything to help?"

"Well, start at the corner there and look through every book on the shelves. If you find any piece of paper at all, or any handwriting in the books, let me see it," Jason Bond told them.

So the real work began on the search for the important paper.

"Thy rod and thy staff they comfort me—"

Chapter 7 / Search for the Will

The search for the will was more involved than anyone had dreamed. Jason Bond and the two girls covered every inch of the house—except the tunnel. The missing key had not been found either, after it had disappeared from Mandie's bureau.

Mandie spoke to Mr. Bond about it, "I've asked Aunt Lou, Liza, Jenny, and even Abraham, and nobody has seen a key of any kind."

"Could be that Mr. Bayne Locke has been in your room, Mandie, but don't ask him about it. We don't want him involved in what we're doing around here. The less he knows the better," Jason Bond told her. "You two girls just keep your eyes peeled. Maybe it'll turn up somewhere."

No one had been able to find the entrance to the tunnel from the inside of the house, and with the key lost, the door could not be opened from the outside.

Mr. Bond was leaving the dining room after breakfast one morning, when there was a knock on the front door. He went to see who it was, followed closely by the two girls.

A tall, middle-aged woman with gray, staring eyes, and a tall, brunette girl were standing there.

"I'm Mrs. Gaynelle Snow and this is my daughter, Ruby. I've come to claim my part of my uncle's estate," the woman announced to Mr. Bond.

"Well, dad-blast it! If everyone in the continent ain't gonna try to claim John Shaw's property!" he shouted angrily.

"What did you say?" The woman stared at him with her sharp eyes, then peered to get a glimpse of Mandie and Polly behind him in the hall. "*Well,* if you're not going to invite me in, I guess I'll just walk in!" She pushed the old man aside and stepped into the hallway. "Where are the servants? Tell one of them to show me to my room!"

"Room! You'd think we was running a hotel here!" Mr. Bond stood there ruffling his white hair, trying to resolve the situation.

Liza was crossing the hall just then and the woman, followed by her daughter, yelled at her, "Hey, you there, find me a room in this mansion!"

Liza stopped and stared at the woman and the girl and then looked at Mr. Bond.

"Might as well take them up to a room," he sighed. "Claim they're kinfolk. I'll have to prove them a lie before I can throw them out."

The girl turned her nose up at Polly and Mandie as she followed Liza and her mother up the stairs.

"Stupid ain't the word!" Polly exclaimed.

"Right you are!" Mandie agreed.

After the unexpected arrival of Mrs. Gaynelle Snow and her daughter, Ruby, things took on an even livelier pace at the John Shaw house.

Mandie and Polly took the notion to move into a bedroom on the third floor. They had grown tired of the room on the second floor where Bayne Locke always seemed to be lurking in the hallway watching their every move. Jason Bond warned they would be too frightened up there and wouldn't stay one night, if that long. But they in turn said they would stay no matter what happened.

Polly's mother, young, widowed, and longing for companionship, saw her chance for a trip to Philadelphia without her daughter, as long as the mystery seemed to be prolonged. Polly eagerly moved more of her things over to join Mandie in their new room on the third floor. Liza thoroughly cleaned the large bedroom for them, but was anxious to get back downstairs. All the servants were leery of the third floor and the attic.

The two girls were putting their things away in the drawers and the wardrobe, when Polly handed Mandie a cut glass jar full of powder. "Here's your powder, Mandie." Just as she reached for it, it slipped and fell to the floor, sprinkling the carpet and dusting Snowball, who gingerly jumped across the room, shaking his feet and licking his fur.

Mandie and Polly were doubled up in giggles at Snowball's action, when Mandie suddenly bent closer to the floor. "Hey, look! The key! Here's the key to the tunnel!" She picked it up from the carpet.

"The key to the tunnel!" exclaimed Polly. "You mean it was in the powder jar?"

"It must have been, it's right here in this pile of powder," Mandie told her. "I wonder where Liza got this jar, anyway."

And at that precise moment, Liza came through the doorway, carrying an armful of Mandie's belongings.

"Say, Liza, where did you get this jar of powder?" Mandie questioned, holding up the jar.

"Land sakes! You done went and spilled powder all over this here rug just after I cleaned it! Now why you want to do that?" Liza scolded her as she dropped the things onto the bed and stood there staring at the powder on the carpet.

"Sorry, Liza, it was an accident," Mandie told her, "but look what was in this jar—the key we've been looking for! Where did you get the jar, Liza?"

"Now let me see," she pondered. "I think it was on the bureau in the room that Mr. Locke is staying in. Yes, that's where it was," Liza went on. "I didn't think he needed that good-smelling powder, so I took it for you."

"Liza!" Mandie laughed. Then she turned to Polly. "Then Bayne Locke must have taken it from my room—the key, that is."

"I didn't think we could trust that man," Polly added.

"Hey, come on. Let's find Mr. Jason and take him to the tunnel," Mandie excitedly brushed the white powder off her skirt. "Let's go!"

They found Mr. Bond on the front porch.

"The key! We found the key! Let's go to the tunnel!" Mandie called as she and Polly ran on down the steps. Mr. Bond scratched his head and followed.

Breathlessly, the two girls pushed aside the bushes in front of the door. Mr. Bond reached for the door to unlock it, but it was already unlocked and standing wide open.

"Well, how do you like that?" Mr. Bond said, as he stepped inside.

"Now, we go for miles and miles before we come to the door into the main part of the house," Mandie told him.

And they walked and walked—down halls, up stairs and down again, and no door appeared to lead into the house at all. Instead, they found a panel in the wall slightly ajar.

"Look, that wall is open a little," Mandie whispered.

As Mr. Bond reached to touch it, the panel closed back into place and they could not even tell it had been open at all.

"Well, looks like it's not meant for us to get through," Mr. Bond said.

"I wonder how that panel got loose," Polly speculated.

"You girls probably knocked something loose

on your travels down through here," Mr. Bond laughed.

"Guess we'll just have to go back out the way we came in," Mandie muttered. "But we're not going to give up."

"Nope, we're not," Polly confirmed. "Must be somebody on the other side of that wall, the way it closed so fast, and I know it was open, 'cause I saw it."

"Probably one of those ghosts we've been trying to catch up with," Mandie teased.

"Maybe we can find the other side of this tunnel now that we know the panel opens," Mr. Bond told them.

They left the tunnel the way they had entered. Mr. Bond locked the door and put the key in his pocket.

The three of them went back into the house and were climbing the steps to the third floor when they met Bayne Locke coming down. He grinned at them and would have gone on down the steps, but Mr. Bond stopped him.

"Look here, fellow, where have you been up that way?"

"Why, I've been up to the third floor," Bayne sarcastically replied. "Where'd you think I'd been?"

"What reason did you have to go up to the third floor?" Mr. Bond wanted to know.

"Hey, mister, you just work here. I am the nephew of the man who owned this house." Bayne was not grinning any longer.

"And I also happen to be in charge of Mr. Shaw's affairs until the will is located," Mr. Bond replied.

At that moment, Mrs. Snow and Ruby appeared at the top of the stairs to the third floor.

Mandie turned to them, "And what were you doing on the third floor?"

Mrs. Snow hurried down the steps, with her daughter at her heels. "What business is it of yours? I have as much right as you do to this house and everything in it. So, don't bother asking me any questions, because you certainly won't get any answers." She kept right on going down to the second floor, her daughter following and turning to make faces at the girls.

"That woman is no relative of mine!" Bayne Locke loudly proclaimed.

The woman turned back. "And Mr. Locke is no relative of mine." She and her daughter disappeared down the hallway below.

"Well, why don't you throw her out? She's certainly not kin to John Shaw!" assured Mr. Locke.

"Same reason I'm not throwing you out right now. I have to prove you're no kin before I can oust you from this house. But that day will come. You can be sure of that." Mr. Bond passed the younger man and went on up the stairs, Mandie and Polly following.

"Guess we won that time," Mandie remarked.

"Yeh, but who's gonna win the final say-so?" Polly replied.

They climbed the stairs all the way to the attic. It was dark and spooky, even though there were gabled windows to let in the daylight. The floor was covered with boxes, old furniture, trunks, dishes, clothes, and even an old organ.

"Now, the best thing to do is to go around the wall like this and tap on it to see if it will move," Mr. Bond told them as he rapped the wooden wall with his hand. "You two go around that way and I'll go this way."

Mandie and Polly did as he told them, laughing as they went, banging on the wall. They were almost all the way around the attic when they realized Mr. Bond was no longer with them.

"Polly! Mr. Bond! He's gone!" Mandie cried. "Where did he go?"

"I don't know. He was here just a minute ago. Maybe he's behind some of that old furniture. You go that way and I'll go this way and maybe we can find him," Polly told her.

As they worked their way around the room, they kept calling, "Mr. Bond! Mr. Bond! Where are you?"

Finally they met again.

"He's not here!" Mandie gasped.

At that moment, something scampered across the floor and both the girls screamed.

"Let's get out of here!" Polly shouted, running for the door to the steps. Mandie, her heart pounding, followed close on her heels, and then she stopped suddenly as she looked back and saw

Snowball beating an old piece of wood around with his paws.

"Oh, Snowball! Polly, it was Snowball!" She picked up the kitten.

"Well, anyway, let's get out of here!" Polly ran ahead to the door.

They came down the steps into the front hall so fast they almost collided with Liza who was passing through with her arms full of bed linens.

"Hey, where you two going?" Liza stepped out of their way just in time.

"Liza, have you seen Mr. Bond? He disappeared," Mandie told her.

"I ain't seed him since he went up the steps with you two," Liza answered. "Why? What's wrong? Something wrong?"

Mandie immediately tried to compose herself, knowing the black girl would become frightened if they told her what had happened.

"Oh, nothing, we just missed him, I guess," Mandie said.

"Yeh, we stayed too long in the attic," Polly helped out.

"You been in the attic? Lawsy mercy, what you two done been doin' in that spooky place?" Liza's eyes widened. "Ain't you'ns askeered to go up there?"

"We just went up there looking for something, Liza. Come on, Polly, let's go out in the yard."

Once the two girls were out of Liza's sight they ran for the entrance to the tunnel.

"He's gotta be in the tunnel. He must've found the panel that opened up," Polly declared.

"Right. Maybe we can find the way in from the tunnel now," Mandie said as she ran on ahead and pushed at the door. "Oh, no, Mr. Bond locked it when we left, remember? And we don't have the key!"

"Guess we give up and go home and wait for him to come back from wherever he's gone," Polly lamented.

To their amazement, Mr. Bond was sitting in the swing on the front porch when they came around the corner of the house.

"Mr. Jason! Where did you go?" Mandie ran to him.

"Where did I go?" the old man asked.

"Yes, when we were in the attic, you just disappeared," Polly added.

"Oh, the attic—why, I just came on back downstairs."

"But we didn't see you leave," Mandie insisted.

"No, because some of that old furniture is taller than you two, I suppose." He smiled at the girls. "Did you get scared because I left you alone up there?"

"Oh, no, Mr. Jason. We were just trying to find you. We thought maybe you had found the secret panel," Mandie told him.

"The secret panel? Oh, the panel to the tunnel. No, I don't suppose there's an opening into the attic after all," Mr. Bond said.

The two girls looked at him and then at each other and didn't say anything else, but they went on inside the house and up to their room on the third floor.

"I don't believe him!" Mandie was emphatic about it.

"Neither do I!" Polly flopped down beside Mandie on the big bed.

"But why would he lie to us, Polly?"

"Must have a good reason."

"Well, after all, this is my uncle's house and Mr. Jason shouldn't keep secrets from me," Mandie moped.

"Nope."

"Well, don't you have any ideas?"

"I just can't figure this one out, Mandie. Everybody seems to be trying to hide something from everybody else."

"I know. Guess it's the money my uncle has. Money makes people fight sometimes, my father always told me. He always said it was better to be poor. Then you would know who your friends really are."

"Oh, Mandie, I don't agree with that at all. I'd just die if we were poor." Then Polly realized what she was saying. "Sorry, I forgot. I mean, I know you told me how poor your family is. But, anyway, don't you think it's better now, with all those new dresses and so much to eat, and servants to do all the work?"

"Well, I suppose. But look at the difference in

things since Bayne Locke and that Mrs. Snow and her terrible Ruby came here. They're all after my uncle's money!"

"So what are we going to do about Mr. Jason now?"

"I suppose we'll have to watch him now, along with the others."

*"Thou preparest a table before me
in the presence of mine enemies—"*

Chapter 8 / Joe Comes to Visit

The people who sat around the dining table at
mealtime after that acted like enemies. There was
very little conversation between any of the occu-
pants of John Shaw's house.

Mr. Bond tried his best to carry on a conversation at the table one day at dinnertime, but Bayne
Locke and Mrs. Snow and her daughter completely
ignored him. The girls did not talk either, but continued to listen and watch everyone else. Mr. Bond
only got curt answers to any questions he asked in
an attempt to draw the girls out.

"Well, if this ain't the quietest bunch I ever seed
in all my born days," Liza remarked as she brought
in the dessert. "What's the matter—cat got all your
tongues?"

Mandie laughed. "No, Liza, we just can't do two
things at one time. If we're going to eat, we have to

eat, and if we're going to talk, we just can't eat."

"Oh, I sees," Liza smiled at her. "Everybody must be starved to death." She twirled on out of the dining room with her arms full of dishes. "Most nonsense I ever heard of!"

"Well, guess she's right," Mr. Bond remarked, looking straight at the two girls. "But if everyone's starved to death, why is everyone leaving so much food on their plates?"

"Don't include me in that. I eat whatever I'm served," Mrs. Snow haughtily informed him.

"So do I," her daughter piped in.

"I'm always hungry. I always eat anything I can get my hands on," Bayne Locke said. "Food's too good to waste."

"That leaves me to answer, I suppose," Mandie volunteered. "My stomach doesn't feel too well lately. Too much excitement around. Besides, I'm not used to so much food at one meal."

"Well, I think eating is a silly habit and a waste of time when you could be doing something more interesting. Therefore, I only eat enough to keep from starving," Polly told them.

"Maybe the food will taste a little better at suppertime," Mr. Bond said as he rose from the table. "Although I didn't see anything wrong with what we just had."

There was a loud knock on the front door. Everyone was silent and listened. There were indistinct voices in the hall and Liza came hurrying into the dining room.

"Missy, you'se got company—the doctor man and his son," Liza announced to Mandie.

"Joe!" Mandie rushed from the room.

She greeted Dr. Woodard and Joe in the front hallway.

She grasped the old man's hand. "Dr. Woodard, I'm so glad to see you, and you, too, Joe." She turned a little shyly toward the boy. "Seems like ages since I saw y'all. Come on into the dining room and meet everybody. You'll probably want something to eat, anyway."

"Wow! Your uncle sure does have a big house." Joe commented.

"Hope you've been all right, Mandie," the old doctor squeezed her hand.

"Everybody," Mandie addressed all who were still at the table, "these are my friends, Dr. Woodard, and his son, Joe."

Liza was already setting two more plates and she motioned for them to sit down.

"Jason Bond, doctor," Mr. Bond said, shaking his hand heartily. "Sit down, eat. You, too, young fellow." As the two sat down, Mr. Bond resumed his seat. Mandie took her place again, and then introduced each one around the table. "This is my friend, Polly Cornwallis. This is Bayne Locke, Mrs. Snow, and her daughter, Ruby. Now do help yourselves, Dr. Woodard, there's plenty to eat."

"Yes, I can see there is," Dr. Woodard said, piling his plate high, and turning to Joe who kept his eyes glued on Polly. "Joe, dig in, boy."

"Oh, yes, sir," Joe answered and began filling his plate, still stealing glances at Polly who was openly staring at him also.

"Where are you from, Dr. Woodard?" Bayne asked him.

"We live near where Amanda comes from, in Swain County," he answered between mouthfuls of green beans and cornbread. "Had to come to Franklin on some business and just thought we'd drop in to see how she was getting on."

"You know that Uncle John died?" Mandie questioned.

"Died? Why, no, I hadn't heard. When? What happened?" Dr. Woodard asked.

"He died right after I came here," she told him. "He was in Europe."

"It was very sudden, doctor, from what his lawyer told me, and he was buried overseas," Mr. Bond added.

"Well, I'm very sorry to hear that," the doctor replied. "Your ma and sister are fine, Amanda. I saw them at the store yesterday."

"Oh, Dr. Woodard, please don't tell them where I am!" Mandie begged, as she quickly studied the doctor's face. "You—you haven't already, have you?"

"Well, as a matter of fact, I have, Amanda. But, now don't you worry. It's all right with your ma, if you want to stay here—but then, what's going to happen now that your uncle is gone?"

"You *told* her?" Mandie felt betrayed.

"Yes, I had to. There was a posse out looking for you all over Nantahala Mountain after you ran away from the Brysons. Just happened you had written Joe where you were going," Dr. Woodard told her. "I didn't want to, Amanda, but I had to. Those men were wasting their time. But like I said, your ma doesn't care if you stay here. She told me so. Will you stay on here, now that your uncle is dead?"

"Yes, I will," Mandie replied. "Mr. Bayne Locke says he is my uncle's nephew and Mrs. Snow says she is his niece. But, we haven't found the will yet, so we don't know what he left to whom."

"Well, that's a nice kettle of fish. Can't find the will, eh?" The doctor continued eating as he turned to Mr. Bond. "Say he has a will to be found yet?"

"That's right. His lawyer believes it's some-where in this house but we haven't turned it up yet," Jason Bond told him. "And until we do, nothing can be settled."

Dr. Woodard turned to Bayne Locke and Mrs. Snow.

"I don't recollect Jim and John Shaw having any other living close relatives," he told them.

"That's because my mother, who was John Shaw's sister, Martha, died when I was born," Bayne told him.

"When you were born? Now, let me see, you must be twenty-two or twenty-three?"

"Twenty-two."

"Well now, twenty-two years ago I was in school

with Jim Shaw and he didn't have a sister. As a matter of fact, I had known the family probably four or five years before that." The doctor was emphatic about this.

"Sorry, but he did have a sister and I am her son," Bayne Locke smiled crookedly at the doctor.

The doctor grunted his disapproval and turned to Mrs. Snow. "And you claim to be a niece? He didn't have any niece except Amanda here."

"Well, I don't know who you think you are, but I guess I know who I am." Mrs. Snow jumped up from the table and threw down her napkin. "Come on, Ruby, we have things to do." And they left the room in a hurry.

"Guess she's mighty sensitive about it," Dr. Woodard mumbled.

"You're absolutely right, Doc," Jason Bond told him. "I know these people are not kin to John Shaw, none of them excepting Amanda here, but I got to get proof before I can put them out. And that proof should be on the way any day."

Mandie finally noticed that Joe and Polly were staring at each other. Thinking they were both just being shy, she tried to start a conversation. "Joe, you just ought to see all the nice clothes Aunt Lou has made for me since I came here."

"Clothes? Aunt Lou? Oh, yes," Joe turned and smiled at her. "I see you have on a new frock. It's awfully pretty."

"Joe, maybe Dr. Woodard would let you visit with us for a while. We have this huge house with all these rooms and all this food," Mandie began.

"Could I, Dad?" Joe turned to his father and watched Polly out of the corner of his eye. "Could I stay here till you come back next week? Please?"

"Well, I don't know about that. There isn't any—"

"Please, Dr. Woodard!" Mandie begged.

Jason Bond tried to help her. "He's welcome, Doc, if he wants to stay. Like Amanda said, plenty of room and plenty to eat."

"What about clothes? What did you bring with you?" his father asked.

"You said we were going to be in Franklin two or three days, so I brought a change of everything," Joe replied. "Please, Dad."

"All right. I'm not sure what your mother will say, but I reckon it'll be all right," his father finally agreed.

"Whee!" Polly spoke at last and jumped up. "Let's show Joe around—all over—you know."

Mandie understood the "all over" to include the tunnel and she quickly left the room with them.

Joe, who inadvertently found himself between the two girls, was speechless with all the finery and rooms in the house, and most of all, the story about the tunnel. Mr. Bond still had the key and Mandie had to return to secretly ask him for it. He smiled and handed it to her.

Curious about the tunnel, Joe was glad that his father had allowed him to stay to visit; but Mandie wanted to talk to him alone and it was near suppertime before she had a chance. Mr. Bond went with Polly to her house next door to get more clothes and Mandie promptly asked Joe to sit in the swing on the front porch with her.

"I sure miss school, with you and everything, Joe," she told the boy.

"Me, too, Mandie. I never go over to your mother's house anymore, but I heard that Irene is getting seriously involved with Nimrod," Joe told her.

"Nimrod! Oh, well, they are two of a kind!" she laughed. "Joe, have you—do you ever—that is, were you ever up at my father's grave since I left?"

Joe reached over and took her hand in his. "Yes, I've been up there several times when I was with Dad in the neighborhood. I've tried to keep it cleaned off. And once in a while, I find some flowers growing along the way and I put them on his grave."

"Thank you, Joe!" She reached over and kissed him on the cheek. "You're the only real friend I ever had."

Joe blushed and squeezed her hand. "You, too, Mandie. You know, we will grow up someday. And I still plan on looking out for you."

"Oh, Joe!" Mandie became shy.

Polly came around the corner of the house suddenly and broke the spell.

"Goodness gracious! Holding hands!" she teased, as she stood in front of them.

Mandie and Joe both blushed then and the boy

nervously watched Polly as she went into the house. Mandie caught the look and sensed some feeling between Joe and her friend, and wise beyond her years, did not give away the fact that she was upset over it. After all, Joe was going to be around until the next week. And after all, she had known Joe all her life and she was sure she came first with him.

Chapter 9 / Uncle Ned's Message

The messenger Mr. Bond had sent to Lawyer Wilson's office returned early one morning, tied his horse to the hitching post at the road and came to the door to give his report.

"Morning, Jason," he said as Mr. Bond opened the door. "I jest got back and came straight hyar."

"Come in, Daniel," Mr. Bond greeted the man. "Come on into the kitchen and I'll see if we can't rustle up a cup of coffee."

"That would be nice, Jason," Daniel said, following him into the kitchen where Jenny, the cook, was washing the breakfast dishes.

"How about some coffee and something to eat with it for my friend here, Jenny? We'll just sit right here," Mr. Bond told her as they sat down at the table where the hired help ate their meals.

"Sho, Mr. Jason, comin' right up," Jenny said, bustling about.

100

"Did you have a good trip, Daniel?" Jason asked, as the man eyed the food being placed before him.

"Well, Tiddlywinks throwed a shoe smack-dab in front of old man George's mansion and that was lucky 'cause his smithy put on a new 'un right then and thar. Otherwise, I tended to my bisness and had to wait fer Lawyer Wilson to come back to town," Daniel told him. "Then when he did git back, didn't do no good. He ain't never heerd of this hyar man, Locke, or that thar woman, Snow. Said they probably thought they could worm their way into some easy money."

"Well, that's exactly what I figured. I didn't believe a word of their stories. Now, what did he say I should do about it?" Jason Bond asked.

"Hyar, he writ you a letter." Daniel pulled out a folded envelope from his shirt pocket.

Jason took it, withdrew a letter on the lawyer's stationery, and read parts of it out loud. " 'Just leave things alone for the time being and I will begin a thorough investigation in order to get the proof we will need to evict them from John Shaw's house.' "

"Sounds like you gonna hafta put up with 'em a whit longer, eh?" Daniel gulped down the last of the strong coffee.

"I 'spec so. We'll have to do things legal-like so there won't be no repercussions," Jason agreed. "Dad-gum, I was hoping I could put them out in the street when you got back. Well, reckon I'll have to wait."

"They been causin' you any trouble?" Daniel asked.

"Not really. It's just that I don't trust them and I can't keep them in my sight all the time."

"Does the girl keep a lookout on 'em, too?"

"Yeh, Mandie and Polly follow them around some—that is, when they're around. I sorta figure Mandie has decided not to trust *me* either. She won't talk about things anymore. And we've got Doc Woodard's boy staying here for a few days from over in Swain County. The girls are more interested in him right now than in our impostors."

"Well, I gotta be ramblin' on home 'fore Sadie hyars I'm done back and ain't come home yit." Daniel rose and turned to Jenny. "Thet was right good, Jenny—good food."

"Yessuh," Jenny replied, smiling.

"You comin' back to town on Saturday?" Jason asked as he led the way to the front door.

"Yeh, reckon I'll have to git some things from the store," Daniel answered, walking on out to his horse.

"Stop by and I'll have the money then to pay you for the trip," Jason told him.

Daniel waved and was off down the road on his horse.

Mandie and Polly came out the front door while Jason still stood there on the porch. Joe was close behind them.

"Well, I see Mr. Daniel got back," Mandie remarked.

"Yep, and Lawyer Wilson don't know nothing atall about these people we got staying here," Mr. Bond told her.

"Does that mean you can make them leave?" Polly asked.

"Nope, he's got to do some investigatin' first."

"Well, I hope it won't take long," Mandie said.

Mandie remembered this was the night that Uncle Ned was supposed to return with his information on the Snows and Bayne Locke. She also knew tomorrow was the day that Polly's mother was supposed to return home, and she was glad because jealousy had sprung up between the two girls over Joe. Not a word had been said, but each one sensed it. Mandie had been subconsciously possessive of Joe from the first day he had smiled at her, and she always felt he had eyes for her only.

Joe was attracted to Polly, but he did his best to remain loyal to Mandie. Polly was attracted to Joe and did nothing to disguise the fact.

"We're going over to my house, Mr. Jason. Mother is coming home tomorrow and I have to tell the cook," Polly told him, as the three went on down the front steps.

"Well, be sure you get back in time for supper," the old man called after them.

Polly bounded along the lane to her house. "Can't wait to see what Mother brings me."

"Is this the first time your mother ever went off and left you?" Joe asked.

"She didn't exactly leave me. I didn't want to go, so I persuaded her to let me stay with Mandie. I've always gone on trips with my mother, but this time I just didn't want to go. Too many interesting things going on," Polly told him. She turned to Mandie. "We sure fell down on our job of finding the will, didn't we?"

"Yeh, but it's bound to be somewhere. It will eventually be found," Mandie said.

"If we could only find the way into the tunnel from inside the house!" Polly sighed.

"Let's try again tonight. Three heads are better than two," Joe suggested.

"All right, except it'll have to be real late, because Uncle Ned is coming as soon as it gets dark," Mandie warned.

"Uncle Ned is coming? How do you know?" Joe asked.

"Because I sent him to Richmond to find out about Bayne Locke and this is the night he said he'd be back. He never fails to keep his word," Mandie assured him.

"Can I see him, this time? Please?" begged Polly. "You always tell me about him but I've never seen him."

"Oh, he's just a real old Indian," Joe told her.

"He's also kin to me somehow. I told you I'm part Cherokee," Mandie put in.

"That's right. I forgot you're an Indian papoose," teased Joe.

"That's not funny, Joe," Mandie snapped.

"Sorry, Mandie, I didn't mean any harm. It's just that I can't get used to the fact that your father was half Cherokee," he said, taking her hand in his, causing her heart to flutter.

"Well, you didn't answer my question. Can I see this kinfolk of yours, Mandie?" Polly tried to break the mood.

"I guess so. But you'll have to wait until I talk to him and tell him you want to meet him. Otherwise he'll run away if someone besides me shows up."

"Well, here we are," Polly said, as the huge house she lived in came into view behind the trees. "Come on, we'll beat Cook out of something good to eat."

Mandie met Uncle Ned that night in the summerhouse after dark, while Joe and Polly waited in the swing on the front porch.

"Uncle Ned, I knew you would come. You always do," she greeted the old man as he appeared from behind the big walnut trees shadowing the porch. "Sit down, Uncle Ned."

The Indian sat across from her and smiled. "Papoose have visitor, doctor son?"

"How did you know?" Mandie asked, smiling.

"Cherokee knows all," the old Indian told her. "Cherokee find people named Locke in big city."

"In Richmond?"

"In Richmond. People know Bayne Locke. People *not* know if Bayne Locke kin to John Shaw."

"They don't?"

"Cherokee stay in Richmond. Find people who know. Then I tell Papoose," Uncle Ned told her.

"So he did come from Richmond and he has relatives there. Well, at least we know that much," Mandie said.

"Must go now. Morning Star send love to Papoose,"he said.

"Give her my love, too, Uncle Ned. But, before you go, please, wait a minute." Mandie grasped his arm as he rose. "My friend, Polly Cornwallis, wants to meet you. She and Joe are on the front porch. Is it all right if I bring them out here to see you?"

"Yes, but hurry," he grunted.

Going around the corner of the house, she beckoned to the two and they came hurrying toward her.

"Polly, this is Uncle Ned," Mandie proudly introduced him. "And Uncle Ned, you know Joe already."

Joe nodded and held out his hand to Uncle Ned. The Indian solemnly shook hands with a grunt.

Polly smiled up at the tall Indian. "How do you do, Uncle Ned? I've heard so much about you that I wanted to meet you."

"Pleased to see Papoose number two," the old man said.

Everyone laughed at his name for Polly. The sound carried to the house. Jason Bond stuck his head out of the upstairs window directly above.

"What's going on down there?" he yelled.

"Nothing, we're just getting some fresh night air," Mandie quickly replied, looking up at him.

At the sound of the other man's voice, Uncle Ned darted out of sight, whispering as he went, "Must go. See Papoose next moon."

Mandie silently waved to him as he disappeared into the shadows.

The three walked back to the front porch and sat down in the swing.

"Say, that was close, Mandie," Joe sighed.

"Sure was, but somehow I don't believe Mr. Jason would mind if I had an Indian friend—unlike the Brysons, who were out to kill every Indian they could find."

There was a slight stirring in the doorway behind them.

"No, I don't mind, Mandie," Mr. Bond said. "I see him every time he comes. And I know who he is."

"Oh, Mr. Jason, you scared me," was all Mandie could say.

"I'm sorry, didn't mean to frighten you. Did he get any information for you?"

"Well, how did you know that?" Mandie was surprised.

"I heard you talking to him the night you asked him to find out about these people," the old man said.

Mandie dropped her voice to a whisper and told him what the Indian had told her.

"That's good. I'll let Lawyer Wilson know. Now

are y'all going upstairs? The parties in question are already turned in for the night."

"Let's do," Polly said.

"Sure, Mr. Jason. We haven't given up. We're going to look upstairs again for an entrance to the tunnel," Mandie chirped.

"Well, get to it then. I'm going back to my room. See you tomorrow." And he disappeared back into the dark hallway.

"Well, what are we waiting for?" Joe laughed.

The three softly crept up the steps to the third floor on their unending mission, being careful not to be heard by their mysterious visitors.

"My cup runneth over—"

Chapter 10 / The Secret Door

Joe led the way, carrying an oil lamp, Mandie close behind with matches in her pocket in case it went out. Polly brought up the rear as they noiselessly tiptoed on up the steps to the attic. Even the old door cooperated by not creaking this time when Joe pushed it open. They moved very slowly and carefully around, whispering softly to each other as they made an inspection of the attic. Joe, still in the lead, held the lamp at arm's length, the light picking up the debris, as the girls closely peered at everything in their path.

Joe carefully inspected the walls and the ins and outs of the eaves and the dormer windows.

"It seems to be awfully solid. I don't see how this wall could open up anywhere and there isn't room for any steps behind it," Joe whispered to the girls.

"But, it has to open somewhere," Mandie insisted.

"Well, look at it. You can see the wall all the way around the house up here, except where it goes into the eaves and the eaves are not high enough to have steps going down," he insisted.

"All right, maybe that's the way it looks, but there's sure an opening somewhere because we found it on the other side in the tunnel," Polly told him.

"Well, if you want to, we can keep moving and check the wall out all the way around," Joe said.

The three silently pushed on the wall as they went, reaching high and low, examining every foot of it. They were all tense with the spooky atmosphere when suddenly there was a loud noise on the third floor.

"Sounds like someone is below us!" Mandie whispered.

"Could be that Mr. Locke or Mrs. Snow," Polly added.

"Come on, let's slip up on them and see who it is," Joe suggested, as he moved toward the door to the steps. "Stay close behind me, because I'm going to blow out the light."

"All right," Mandie said softly, as she and Polly held hands and Joe put out the lamp.

They felt their way down the dark steps to the door leading into the hall of the third floor. Joe put out his hand to caution them to be quiet as he slowly pushed the door open. It was still dark on the third floor hallway and there was no sign of a light or anyone around.

Mandie pulled at Joe's shirt. "Psst! Go left toward Uncle John's library."

Joe followed her directions and the three slipped along the passageway to the door of the library Mr. Bond had shown them the other day. As they reached it they heard a slight movement in the room.

"There's someone in there!" Joe whispered, putting his hand on the doorknob, the girls close behind him.

"Push it open," Mandie urged him.

With that, the three burst into the room which was in total darkness. A man's figure outlined by the moonlight from the window moved quickly toward the small door that had been locked the day Mr. Bond was with them, and to which no one had the key. Just as the figure reached the door, the three dived at him, pulling him to the floor.

"All right, we've got you!" Joe cried, as he held onto the man's coattail. The girls were snatching for his sleeves and kicking him in the shins.

"Hey, wait a minute! Let's get some light in here!" the man said quickly.

"No!" Joe shouted. "Here, Mandie, take the lamp and light it. I'll hold onto him!"

The man quit struggling and Mandie quickly lit the lamp with a match from her pocket. Then, holding the lamp, she stared into the man's face, her hand shaking violently.

"Oh, no!" she cried, unable to move.

"Mandie!" the man said, smiling at her.

"You can't be my Uncle John!" Mandie shook her head.

The man reached for her and took her into his arms as he passed the lamp on to Joe.

"But, I am!" He kissed her hair. "My dear little niece!"

"Then, you really are my Uncle John?" Mandie's voice trembled with excitement.

"Yes, I guess I played a mean trick on you," he told her.

Joe and Polly stood there staring and listening.

"But, Mandie, how do you know this man is your Uncle John? You said you had never seen him," Joe insisted.

"Yes, it is Mr. Shaw, Joe. My next-door neighbor, remember?" Polly assured him.

"He's just like my daddy! Can't you see that, Joe? You knew my daddy. He looks just like him, except maybe a little older." She leaned back to gaze into the smiling face—so familiar, yet different.

"Good guess. I'm fifteen years older," Uncle John said.

"But why did you make us think you were dead, Mr. Shaw?" Joe asked.

"Well, I guess I just wanted to see what would happen to my property when I do die. When I heard of my brother Jim's death, it was too late to see him, of course, but, thank the Lord, I had written him a letter before he died," he said, sitting down at the desk. "You see, there's been hard feelings between the two of us since before you were born, Amanda. Then when I learned that he—was gone, I knew you were my only living relative, and since you are so young, I had to find out just whom I could trust to look out for you if anything happened to me."

"Then Bayne Locke and the Snows are no kin to you?" Mandie sat on the floor at his knee, while Joe and Polly hovered nearby fascinated with their discovery.

"Absolutely none! And I want them out of my house immediately! I had to take my lawyer into my confidence to send the message of my demise and of course he knows they are no kin, but he would have to prove it to stand up in court."

"But, Uncle John, where have you been all this time?" Mandie wanted to know. "That is, since I've been here."

"I've been living with my people—the Cherokees." He smiled at the girl. "Remember, we *are* part Cherokee."

"You've been living with the Cherokees? Then Uncle Ned must have known all along what was going on!" she reasoned.

"Yes, I came home with him when he saw you out in the yard earlier tonight. I could see things were getting out of hand, with no one able to find my will and all. However, I didn't know you children were occupying rooms on the third floor, and you almost caught me when you got the lamp from Amanda's room and went to the attic."

"Well, where is that will?" Polly put in.

"It's under the carpet over there by the door," he said, pointing toward the small door which was still closed.

"Under the carpet?" All three gasped and then laughed.

"What a good place to hide it!" Joe exclaimed.

"Where does the door lead to, Uncle John?" Mandie questioned. "Mr. Jason tried to open it, but it was locked and he didn't have the key."

"Oh, he has no idea where that door leads. He has never had a key. I have the only key." He pulled it from his pocket and got up to walk to the door. "Here, you want to see what's behind here?"

Mandie scrambled after him, Polly and Joe crowding closely behind her. John Shaw put the key in the lock, turned it with a click, and pushed open the door. Behind it was a paneled wall. Reaching to one side he pushed a latch and one panel swung aside. And there before them was the entrance to the tunnel.

He smiled as the three gasped in surprise.

"Uncle John!" Mandie covered her mouth with her hands.

"If we only could have found a way to unlock that door!" Polly moaned.

"And all this time you have been trying to open a wall in the attic!" Joe laughed.

"The tunnel stops here. It doesn't go up to the attic," Uncle John told them.

"But, what is the tunnel for?" Mandie asked.

"My grandfather, your great-grandfather, Amanda, who was also named Jim Shaw, built this house at the time the Cherokees were being run out of North Carolina. He didn't believe in the cruel way the Indians were being treated and he had this tunnel built for them. He hid dozens of Cherokees in there, fed and clothed them, and then helped them on their way when things calmed down along about 1842, and they could set up living quarters somewhere else," John Shaw told her. "That was the way my father met my mother. He was twenty-eight years old and had never been married when he met my mother. She was only eighteen, a beautiful young Indian girl."

"She was beautiful, Uncle John?" Mandie grasped his hand.

"Very beautiful, Amanda. I have her portrait. The frame needed redoing. It's in Asheville now, being refinished. You'll see it when it comes back."

"Oh, Uncle John, I'm so happy!" Tears filled Mandie's eyes as she looked up into her uncle's face. "I'm so happy you are—not—are still alive!"

At that moment, there was the sound of footsteps in the hall. Jason Bond appeared in the doorway and almost dropped the lamp he was carrying when he saw John Shaw standing there.

"Mr.—Mr.—S-Shaw!" he stammered.

"Yes, it's me, Jason. Sorry I couldn't let you in on the secret, but no one knew I was really and truly alive except Ed Wilson," John Shaw told him. "And I must say you've played your part well, Jason. You can be trusted." John Shaw explained everything to Jason Bond, who still stood there gaping and trembling.

"Oh, dear," Jason muttered as he learned the truth. "I—I'm sure glad you're back, Mr. Shaw. It sure straightens out a lot of problems. Like these people that moved in here—"

"Yes, I know. I knew about them as soon as they arrived. Uncle Ned kept me informed as to what was going on. Sorry you had to put up with them, but as soon as the sun rises they will be hitting the road."

And that was the way it happened. Upon being confronted by the real, living John Shaw, Bayne Locke, Mrs. Snow and her daughter were all too glad to pack up their belongings and leave the next morning.

Mandie stood on the porch holding her uncle's hand as the three made their abrupt exit. She breathed a sigh of relief.

"Now maybe things will simmer down!" she exclaimed.

"Well, no, actually things are just beginning to happen! I'm expecting company from Asheville." He squeezed her hand.

Joe and Polly, standing nearby, looked at each other and Polly said, "Well, my mother is coming home today. So that eliminates one more guest from this house."

Joe scratched his head. "Don't know when

Dad will come back for me, but it should be sometime this week."

John Shaw turned to them and said, "Well, let's not everybody leave at once! I thought we could have a little party when the company arrives from Asheville."

The three young people grinned at each other. *A party? What fun!* Mandie had not the faintest idea as to the importance of the party or the people who would be visiting. She merely knew it would be her very first *real* party.

"Surely goodness and mercy shall follow me all the days of my life—"

Chapter 11 / The Truth Revealed

The return of John Shaw was truly a happy event in the household. Every piece of furniture in the house was polished, silverware was cleaned, the best linens laid out for use, and two guest rooms readied for the two mysterious visitors who were coming from Asheville.

Mandie moved back to her room on the second floor. Joe also moved his things down to a room on the same floor. Everyone was excited, but no one could find out the names of the expected guests and John Shaw remained secretive about the whole thing.

Polly's mother returned and Polly moved back home, but came to visit Mandie every day. Joe received a note from his father saying there was a sudden outbreak of fever and he was needed so badly he couldn't come for him until things were under control.

Early one bright, sunshiny morning John Shaw drew Mandie off into the parlor.

"Today is the day the company's coming. Now, I want you to put on your loveliest dress and brush your hair until it shines—that is, if it will shine any more than it does already."

"Oh, Uncle John, I'm *so* excited! I don't even know these people, but I'll do my best to look and act like a lady," she promised him.

"That's all I ask, and I know you will." The old man smiled and her heart melted as the memory of her father's smile flooded back to her.

Mandie hurried off to her room and enlisted the aid of Liza to button her up in the newest dress that had been made for her. It was made of snow-white muslin covered with sprigs of bluebells that matched her blue eyes. Liza combed out her long blonde hair and let it hang loose in ringlets.

"Miss Amanda, you are really and truly beautiful today," Liza said, admiring the finished product.

Mandie laughed nervously. "Why do you say that, Liza, because you made me that way with all your fussing?"

"Nope, you just got that natural bloom today. Wouldn't doubt but that Joe boy tries to put some sugar on them lips if he catches you by yourself," Liza teased her.

Mandie blushed. "Oh, Liza, quit that silly talk. You know Joe has been my friend all my life. But, he's *not* my boyfriend."

"No, he ain't no boyfriend yet, but I can tell he'd *like* to be," Liza answered solemnly. "One of these days you'll know."

"Do you really think so, Liza?" Mandie turned to stare at the black girl.

"Sho as I'm astandin' here." Liza crossed her arms over her bosom. "You wait and see. And 'member I told you so."

Mandie's cheeks were still rosy. "Liza, do you think Uncle John will approve of the way I look?"

" 'Course he will. Now, you'd best be gittin' on down there to the parlor and act like a lady. Company comin' any minute now." Liza hurried her down the steps to the parlor where Uncle John was waiting.

"Where's Joe? Isn't he dressed yet?" Mandie looked around.

"First of all, my dear niece, you are absolutely lovely," her uncle told her. "As for Joe, I sent him on an errand. He won't be back for a while."

"Oh," was all she could say. She had been counting on Joe's support at her side to meet these important strangers who were coming to visit.

At that moment, there was the sound of creaking wagon wheels and horses stopping out front, and John Shaw turned quickly to her. "Supposing you wait right here, my dear. I'll meet the company at the door and bring them in to meet you shortly."

"Yes, sir, Uncle John," she agreed and he quickly left the room.

Mandie could hear women's voices at the door,

one sounded older and one quite young; there was also the soft speech of a black woman, and Aunt Lou was directing them inside with the baggage.

"John Shaw, you could give a person more time to get things together for such a trip," the younger voice was teasingly greeting Mandie's uncle.

"My, yes, you'd think someone was dying, instead of it being a party we are coming to," agreed the older woman.

"Well, I think you'll find the party well worth your sudden trip. Come on in here to the parlor. I want you to meet my other guest," John Shaw was saying.

"Really, John, we should freshen up a bit first," the younger woman was hesitating.

"Nonsense, you never looked lovelier. Come on," he insisted.

John Shaw appeared at the doorway to the parlor, accompanied by the most beautiful young woman Mandie had ever seen. She was dressed in rich silks, with diamonds sparkling on her fingers, and the scent of perfume came with her into the room. She had piles of shining golden hair, sparkling blue eyes, and a complexion that looked as though it had never been exposed to the sun's rays.

Mandie could hardly take her eyes off the younger woman, but snatched a look at the heavy-set, bustling matron, also dressed in the finest and most fashionable clothes Mandie had ever seen.

John Shaw hesitated. "Amanda, this is

Elizabeth—you read about her in my letter to your father that night—"

The young girl was overwhelmed. So, this was the woman who had loved her father. She rushed forward to take her dainty hand. Elizabeth kept staring at Mandie and the older woman caught her breath and stood as if frozen to the spot.

Elizabeth was quite flustered as she turned to John Shaw. "John, who is this girl?"

John Shaw put one arm around Elizabeth and the other around Mandie.

"Elizabeth, this is your daughter, Amanda Elizabeth—"

The young woman trembled violently and John led her to a sofa to sit down, while Mandie, not quite comprehending the situation, trailed along, still holding onto her hand.

"Sorry it had to be such a shock, but I only found out the truth myself just a few months ago," John told her.

The older woman had finally found her voice. "John Shaw, just what kind of trick are you playing?"

"It's no trick, Mrs. Taft. You, of all people, know that. You knew that Elizabeth's baby didn't—"

John was interrupted by Mandie's urgent tugging at his coat. "Uncle John, what—who—"

Elizabeth and Mandie were staring at each other, speechless.

"John, it can't be! You know my baby died," Elizabeth kept repeating. Then she turned to Mandie, "Do you know your birthdate, child?"

"Oh, yes, I was born June 6, 1888," Mandie managed to say.

"Your baby did not die, Elizabeth. This is your baby—grown to a full twelve years old, never knowing who her real mother was," John was telling the young woman.

"John Shaw, you are only making trouble, you know that," Mrs. Taft was warning him as she sank into a deep chair.

"Uncle John, please—" Mandie begged.

"Yes, my child, this *is* your real mother, and this dear woman is you real grandmother," John finally turned to Mandie.

"It is quite a long story. Your mother, Elizabeth Taft, ran away and married your father thirteen years ago, but her parents opposed the marriage because your father was half Indian. Your father had lived here with me before that. Elizabeth's parents managed to have the marriage annulled and moved to Asheville to get away from your father's influence. Then, they discovered Elizabeth to be expecting a child. So, they sent her to an aunt's house in Madison County where you were born. They told your mother you died at birth, and persuaded your father to take you, telling him that Elizabeth had agreed she had made a mistake and didn't even want to see you. Then Jim pulled up stakes—"

"Oh, no, no! It must be a lie! To think my own mother and father could have done such a thing to me!" Elizabeth sobbed.

"Jim took you, Amanda, off to Swain County and had the misfortune of meeting Etta McHan, a widow with a daughter, who immediately latched onto him and got him to the altar. He never came to Franklin again, that I know of. You see, he and I were both in love with Elizabeth and he figured I had a hand in breaking up his marriage, but, so help me God, I never even knew you existed until a few months ago," John Shaw continued.

"That, that—woman—in my father's house—is not my real mother?" Mandie could hardly believe it.

"That's right. Not one whit kin to you, nor is her daughter. And I have Uncle Ned to thank for informing me of your father's death and of your existence. And, Amanda, he did get my letter about Elizabeth before he passed on and after I put two and two together, he wrote me about you."

"Then, you actually didn't know about me, Uncle John?"

"No, not until just before your father passed away. You see, Jim never came back to the house here. He just went off without ever seeing me and I had no idea he had taken a baby with him. I also fell for the lie about your death," her uncle said.

"Honor thy mother," Mandie was mumbling to herself.

Elizabeth, trying to recover from the shock, suddenly stretched out her arms to Mandie. "I've always had a strange feeling—Come to me, my—my daughter!" Mandie rushed into her arms and their tears mingled, as Mandie babbled incoherently, "Oh, Mother, Mother, my very own *real* mother! I'm so, so glad! I'm so happy! Thank you, dear God! Thank you, dear God!"

John Shaw turned to Mrs. Taft who was silently wiping tears from her chubby cheeks. "I'm sorry I had to do that but, but I had to. Let's leave them be, now. Come on, I'll show you to your room where you can be comfortable." He offered his arm and without a word the old lady rose and left the room with him.

"Let me look at my beautiful daughter!" Elizabeth held Mandie at arm's length. "And all those years I've missed being with you. Oh, my baby!" She held Mandie close. "I won't miss another minute away from you. You can be sure of that, my darling. And your father, Amanda—I loved him so much." Tears glistened in her eyes. "It's too late now for that, but it's not too late to claim my own daughter."

"My father never loved that—that woman. I'm sure of that." Mandie told her. "She never loved him either. Oh, *why* didn't my father tell me who my own mother was?"

"Don't blame him, my child. If anyone is to blame, it's myself. I shouldn't have given him up so easily," Elizabeth told her as she stroked the girl's soft, blonde curls. "And believe me, I will never give you up."

"Oh, Mother!" Mandie cried.

"And you know—we have the same name.

Your father named you Amanda Elizabeth, which is my own name. That proves he loved me, doesn't it?"

"Yes, yes, I know he must have loved you, Mother, because he never loved anyone else."

Upon learning who the visitors were, Joe was overwhelmed and Polly could only stare at the beautiful young woman. And Mandie would not let her mother out of her sight, and was reluctant to go to bed that night, even though she would be close by.

Mandie knelt by her bed that night and thanked God. "Oh, God, you are so good to me! I know now that you do love me. All the trials and troubles I had to go through were necessary to bring back my own real mother. Please forgive me for ever doubting that you loved me. I should have remembered— *The Lord is my Shepherd, I shall not want!*' "

And while Amanda tossed and turned in her bed, too excited to go to sleep, John Shaw and Elizabeth Taft were alone in the parlor. Mrs. Taft had retired early, complaining of being tired from her journey, but, actually, glad to get away from the two who had stirred up the secret past.

It had started to rain after supper, and John lit the fire in the parlor to keep out the sudden, damp chill that so often came in the mountains. He and Elizabeth were sitting on a low sofa in front of the fireplace, silently watching the flames jump and sing as they raced up the chimney. Neither had spoken a word after bidding Mandie and Mrs. Taft good night.

Finally, John leaned closer covering her small white hand with his larger rough one. "Elizabeth—"

"Yes, John—" Elizabeth breathed softly, placing her other hand on top of his.

"It's—it's been a long time—" John faltered.

"Too long, John. And even now, Mother didn't want to come to your house. I threatened to make the trip by myself and then she gave in. I really believe she was afraid to face you after all these years," Elizabeth said.

"Well, I imagine she must have realized that somehow your trip here concerned Jim."

"Yes, an old friend of thirteen years ago doesn't just suddenly invite you to 'a most important occasion' at his house without good reason, and what good reason it was, John!" She smiled at him as tears of happiness filled her eyes.

"Elizabeth, I wish I had known the truth years ago. Even though I was in love with you, I would have done anything I could to get you and Jim back together."

"John, I can never thank you enough for giving me back my daughter," she said, squeezing his hand between hers.

John turned to her, "Then, Elizabeth, would you consider sharing her with me, now that—"

"Oh, John, no, don't say that. I don't want to hurt you, but you know how much I loved Jim. I've never looked at another man."

"I know that, Elizabeth. But he was my brother

and he is no longer with us. I would be willing to take a chance because I love you so much."

"But that wouldn't be fair to you—" she hesitated.

"That's for me to decide. It would be enough to know that you were finally mine."

"John, I just don't know. I really am truly fond of you, but in a different way from the way I loved Jim."

"I know that. But, I'm hoping that with time you will love me, too. It would be wonderful to share Amanda with you, too. She is the only living relative I have left, except some distant Cherokee cousins."

Elizabeth was silent for a few moments. "Let me think it over tonight. And I'll see you at breakfast—early," she said, rising as he still held both her hands.

"Fine, Elizabeth. I hope you sleep well and have pleasant dreams of me." He laughed. "I don't imagine you will sleep a wink after all the excitement, but, anyway, you are right. It is time to retire. I'll be up with the birds in the morning, and I hope I have something to sing about." He bent and kissed her lightly on the lips.

Elizabeth looked solemnly up into his face. "Until then, John."

*"And I will dwell in the house of
the Lord forever—"*

Chapter 12 / The Wedding

After hours of tossing, unable to sleep, Mandie
finally slept soundly for two hours then awoke with
a start. She sat straight up in bed, trying to remember what was so special. The first streaks of
light were in the sky and she could hear the twitter-
ing of the birds in the tree outside her window.

Then it suddenly came to her. Her mother—
her real mother—her very own mother was here in
this house!

She bounced out of bed and hastily snatching
clothes from the drawers and the wardrobe she
was quickly dressed. She quietly opened her door
and crept down the long stairway.

The smell of fresh coffee was in the air and she
knew Jenny must be up. Slipping into the kitchen,
she found Aunt Lou busily giving the day's instruc-

tions to Jenny, who was rolling out the dough for the morning's biscuits.

"Aunt Lou, is my mother up yet?" Mandie quickly asked the old woman, who was startled by the sudden presence behind her.

"She ain't been in here if she is, my child," Aunt Lou smiled and put her arm around the girl. "Set yo'self down over there. I'll get fresh milk for you while you wait on dat important lady."

Mandie smiled and sat down at the table. Aunt Lou wiped one hand on her apron and poured a glass of milk from the pitcher on the sideboard.

"Here, you drink this. You ain't et a bite since them people come here. Your stomach's gonna be stuck to your backbone, first thing you know."

Mandie laughed and gulped the milk down. "Thank you, Aunt Lou. My stomach does feel kinda hungry."

Liza breezed into the kitchen. "Lady's in the dining room. Mr. John, too."

Mandie scrambled to her feet and ran for the door, "Oh, I have to go. Thank you, Aunt Lou. Thank you, Liza." Then turning back, she added, "And thank you, Jenny! *Thanks, everybody!*"

She hurried through the door, then slowed down to approach her mother and Uncle John who sat at the table. They both turned to smile at her.

"Good morning, Mother. Good morning, Uncle John," she greeted them, slipping into a chair at the side across from the two of them. The thought of her real mother being present still seemed a bit strange to her.

"Good morning, my darling. I hope you slept well." Elizabeth reached over to pat her hand.

"Good morning, my dear," Uncle John said, watching the two.

"Mother, I thought about it all night last night. Where are we going to live?" Mandie questioned.

"Why, we'll go back to Asheville, of course," Elizabeth told her.

"But, couldn't we stay here with Uncle John? You see, I've just found him, too, and I'd like to get to know him. He looks so much like my father." Mandie looked from one to the other.

"Well, Elizabeth?" John queried.

"Well, John —" the young woman began.

Mandie nervously interrupted. "I was thinking about this so much I couldn't sleep last night and I think I have a good solution to our problem."

"Why, what's that?" Uncle John asked.

"Well, it's like this," Mandie began, and then paused to look from one to the other. "Mother, if you and Uncle John would just get married, then we could all stay together here for always!"

Elizabeth laughed hysterically. "And here I was afraid to express my own mind for fear my daughter wouldn't like it."

John laughed, too. "Has Amanda answered my question, then, Elizabeth?"

Mandie was confused by the conversation, and was trying to figure out what they were talking about, when Elizabeth turned to her daughter. "You see, dear, your Uncle John asked me last night to marry him—"

"He did? Oh, Mother! Oh, Uncle John!" Mandie cried, and got up and ran around to embrace them both.

Elizabeth finished her sentence. "And I told him I had to think about it overnight. I was really afraid you wouldn't approve."

"Oh, Mother, he's my father's brother!" Mandie exclaimed.

"Amanda, my child!" Uncle John got up to put his arms around the girl. She looked up into his face and saw the strong resemblance of her father. She buried her face against his chest.

"You have my answer, John dear," Elizabeth told him.

Just then, Mrs. Taft came through the doorway. Mandie ran to her, grabbing her hand and leading her to the table.

"Guess what, Mrs.—Grandmother—you are my grandmother, you know," she told her as she pulled out a chair across the table from her mother.

"Yes," the old lady grudgingly admitted as she sat down.

"Guess what, Grandmother?" Mandie plopped down beside her. "My mother and my Uncle John are going to get married!"

Mrs. Taft darted a glance at the two. "This is quite sudden, isn't it, Elizabeth?"

"Not as sudden as you think, Mother. You see, John has been asking me to marry him for the last fifteen years, through the mail," Elizabeth told her mother, and winked at John.

"That's right, Mrs. Taft. I never gave up," John laughed.

Mandie cut in. "But it was my idea, really. I told them if they would just get married, then Mother and I could live here. We wouldn't have to go to Asheville."

"Oh—so you won't live in Asheville?" the old lady asked. "Well, Amanda, you haven't seen our home in Asheville yet. Your grandfather was one of the richest men in the country and when he died ten years ago, he left a fortune to your mother and me."

"Oh, that's very nice, Grandmother, but I'd really prefer living here where my father used to live," Mandie told her. She looked around the huge room. "Just think. He used to eat in this very room. Oh, I loved him so much."

Elizabeth turned to her mother. "You don't really need me, Mother. You have all the servants. I think Amanda has a good idea. We'll just live here and be on our own."

"Don't tell me you are allowing a child to make such important decisions for you!" the old lady rebuked her daughter.

"No, Amanda did not make any decisions for me. John asked me last night to marry him and I was ready to say yes this morning, provided we lived in this house. You are welcome to stay, Mother, of course, but this will be our home."

"Well, I was just—I didn't—" the old woman was quite ruffled at having her daughter speak to her in such a way.

"It is better this way, Mrs. Taft," John added. "I would never think of parting with this house. It's to be Amanda's at the time of my death, and I trust she keeps it in the family."

"Have it your way, then. I'll go back to Asheville where I have friends," Mrs. Taft replied curtly, then added, "After the wedding, that is, so I hope you won't delay too long with your plans."

Plans were indeed rapidly made. Dresses were ordered, the house refurbished, and guests invited. Elizabeth insisted on having Uncle Ned come to the wedding. After all, he was kinpeople to her new family.

Dr. Woodard finally came for Joe, but prom-ised to return with Mrs. Woodard for the wedding. Mandie was surprised to learn that Dr. Woodard and her mother seemed to know each other from way back.

Polly and her mother paid them a formal call and Mandie was again surprised to find that Polly's mother also knew her mother from long ago. Actu-ally, Mandie's mother had been born and raised and lived in Franklin until her father moved to Asheville when she was sixteen. And there he had built their mansion.

It seemed to Mandie that everyone in town was talking about the forthcoming wedding and had been invited to attend. Things moved along quickly and the day soon was upon them.

Uncle Ned arrived and was given a guest room,

even though he felt very uncomfortable among the white people. Mandie and Polly were the bride's attendants. Joe and his father stood for Uncle John. The ceremony took place on a warm September afternoon in the chapel of the church across the road where John Shaw was a member and where Elizabeth Taft had belonged before moving out of town.

Everything seemed like a dream to Mandie—all white, full of clouds and scents of flowers, soft music, and whispering voices. Her feet never seemed to touch the floor as she floated down the aisle with her bouquet. She was so happy, she was afraid she would awaken and find it was not true. She faintly heard the wedding march. She barely understood the words of the pastor. And when her mother and her uncle floated back down the aisle together and out through the door of the church, she pinched herself to be sure it was real.

The drawing room of Uncle John's house had been transformed into a wonderland for the reception. There were flowers, greenery, and candles everywhere. Mandie darted in and out through the room to keep from missing anything. She had never known there could be such happiness. She caught a glimpse of her grandmother sitting alone in a corner and tried to talk to her, but the old lady had little to say to anyone except Jason Bond, whom she had charmed.

"Hey, slow down, Mandie," Joe said as he caught her arm at the corner of the long table holding the cake and punch bowl. "Where're you going in such an all-fired hurry?"

"Ain't goin' nowhere," she teased him.

"Ain't goin' nowhere? I think you'd better go somewhere—back to school if that's the way you're going to talk," Joe laughed.

"Oh, yes, I'm going back to school, all the way through, with years and years of education," Mandie continued to joke with him.

"But not *too* many years," Joe said, as he moved closer. "I don't want you to know more than I do."

"Know more than you do?" she asked, twirling her long silk skirts.

"That's right. I don't want my wife to be smarter than I am," he said, reaching to grasp her hand.

"*Wife?*" Mandie shot back.

"You heard right. I said my wife. I'm asking you now to become my wife—that is, when we get all educated and grown up, and all that, of course," he said, looking seriously into her blue eyes.

"Oh, Joe Woodard, you're not old enough to propose," she teased.

"I'm old enough to know what I want," he said. "Well, what is your answer? Will you be my wife— someday?"

Mandie became solemn. "I'll have to think about it, Joe. Too much has happened lately."

"I'll wait for your answer. Whenever you make up your mind let me know," he said, squeezing her hand hard.

"Holding hands in public! Shame! Shame!" Polly appeared at Mandie's side.

"Well, shame on you for being so nosy!" Mandie retorted.

"I have to look where I'm going, don't I? I couldn't just close my eyes as I passed," Polly scolded.

"Let's go talk to Uncle Ned. He looks kinda left out over there in the corner," Mandie remarked, and the three moved across the room to where the old Indian was sitting on a stool quietly taking in the whole scene.

Mandie was so happy she was giddy. As she approached the old man, she laughed, "Uncle Ned, will you come to my wedding? Joe has asked me to marry him!"

Polly stared at Joe in disbelief. Joe blushed and slipped away across the room.

"When Papoose gets to be squaw, then I come to wedding," Uncle Ned smiled.

"Joe!" Mandie called after him. "I didn't mean—don't be angry with me!" But he ignored her and kept going.

"Uncle Ned, I guess I said the wrong thing, but everything is so out-of-this-world right now, I can hardly cope." Mandie put her arm around the old Indian. "I'm so glad you came."

Mandie didn't get a chance to see Joe again, alone, and he and his father left early the next morning. Then she learned that her mother and her new stepfather were going to Swain County to visit her father's grave and his Cherokee kinpeople, and she was to go with them.

Uncle Ned went ahead to prepare the Cherokees for the visit. Mandie still could not comprehend; so much was happening. All her young life she had never known what it was to be really and truly happy. She thanked God every night for being so good to her.

To top off the excitement, they went by train. Mandie had never been inside a real train before. It was stuffy and dirty, but to her it was like a chariot from Heaven. At the station, Dr. Woodard, his wife and Joe met them, and they went to spend the night at their house. Mandie knew she would get a chance to see Joe alone, sooner or later.

After supper, as the older people were sitting around discussing old times, Mandie asked Joe to show her his dog's new puppies. They went outside and into the barn where Samantha was giving her four offspring their supper. She flapped her tail when she saw Joe approaching, but kept right on with her duties. She was a golden brown mixed breed and her puppies were a variety of colors.

"Joe, they are beautiful! But, they're so little! Watch that black one! What a little pig. He keeps rooting the others away," the girl laughed.

"They might let him push and shove, but they get their share," Joe assured her. Then he turned abruptly to her, "Well, did you make up your mind?"

Mandie blushed. "Oh, Joe, I'm really and truly

sorry for the way I acted at the wedding. I was just plain in the clouds during the whole time. I acted so foolishly."

Joe dropped his head and kicked at the straw on the floor. Then he looked straight into her eyes. "That's all right, Mandie. I understand. After all, it isn't every day one finds their real mother and then gets a stepfather, too."

"It's all so unreal," she said quietly.

"But, you still didn't tell me. Did you make up your mind about us?" He was determined.

"I've been thinking about it, Joe. I'll—I'll let you know tomorrow," she promised him.

"All right, tomorrow I'll expect your answer." He turned to the doorway. "Let's go back to the house. I'm hungry. How about you?" He took her hand and they laughed together.

The next day was like opening an old scrapbook and reliving the old memories. They all piled into the Woodards' wagon and began their journey up the mountainside. They approached the cemetery from the opposite side and did not pass Jim Shaw's house.

At the sight of the graveyard, Mandie jumped from the moving wagon and hurried to kneel at her father's grave. There were several withered bunches of wild flowers which Joe, true to his word, had put there. The Woodards stayed in the wagon while John helped Elizabeth down and together they joined Mandie in silence, standing hand in hand, and gazing at the mound of dirt which had settled considerably from the rain.

Mandie's memories of the day of the funeral came flooding back and tears flowed down her cheeks. If only her father could see them all now. She suddenly burst into uncontrollable sobs, and in a flash Joe jumped from the wagon and flew to her side.

Elizabeth blinked back the tears as John squeezed her hand and pulled out a clean white handkerchief, carefully wiping first her tears and then his own.

"We all loved him, John," she whispered as she moved closer.

"Yes, we all loved him, my darling," John replied, holding her tightly.

Joe was whispering. "Mandie, he can't hear you. He's in Heaven."

"I know that! I know that!" she sobbed.

It was a silent group who came down the mountain through Charley Gap in sight of Jim Shaw's house. As soon as she spotted the house, Mandie reached instinctively for Joe's hand.

"Joe, I'll marry you when we get grown, if you'll get back my father's house for me." A sob caught in her throat.

Joe put his arm around her. "I will, I promise I will, Mandie." He roughly planted a kiss on her cheek as the wagon jolted them along the bumpy trail and Amanda slid closer and smiled.

"Guess we'll be seeing your Cherokee kinpeople next," Joe said.

"Yes," Amanda whispered, afraid to breathe for fear she would awaken and find it all a dream. "Thank you, God. Thank you for everything. My cup runneth over." She lifted her face to the morning sun.

Somehow, the secret tunnel back home seemed far away and unimportant.